Lost Memories
AND OTHER THINGS I THOUGHT I FORGOT

N K Hatendi

immortalise

First published in 2022 by Immortalise

contact: info@immortalise.com.au

ISBN   - print: 978-0-6488957-9-4
          - ebook: 978-0-6455379-9-4

To my wonderful daughters Florence, Tendai and Chido

who shared their love and gave me time and support so I could put

pen to paper.

Contents

Till Death Do Us Part

Sekuru and Mbuya's routine had changed very little since their wedding on April Fool's Day in 1961. Their Diamond Jubilee celebration had snuck upon them, and they had no reason to suspect anything when the couple dressed in their Sunday best agreed to go for a ride that afternoon. They envisaged a few drinks, perhaps a dinner at a nearby restaurant and then home. They didn't expect to be driven to a five-star hotel on the outskirts of town and knew something was up when they were greeted by their numerous grandchildren whooping, laughing and milling around the hotel reception. The youngest one, guided by her older sibling, presented Mbuya with a large bouquet of pink roses, nearly squashed as Mbuya smothered the grandchild with kisses and a bear hug.

The concierge observing at a distance was all smiles as he escorted the couple with their grandchildren up a spiral staircase with plush maroon carpets and overhanging chandeliers. Soft music was seeping through from the other side of an imposing pair of oak doors. The excited grandchildren surrounded and escorted the couple into a loud blast of music. Sekuru and Mbuya looked at each other with broad smiles and exclaimed in unison, "Our favourite song!" The two fell into step, swaying to the music as they entered the large ballroom. There was ululating and clapping, and everyone abandoned their four-course place settings to rush and greet the couple. Sekuru smiled continually. His wife, speechless, held a handkerchief over her mouth.

"Mum, Dad, welcome! Come and sit," said Mwadiwa, their eldest son gesturing to an elegant top table across the room. He smiled and hugged his new and newly pregnant wife. "You look genuinely surprised! Come, come, we were waiting for you, our guests of honour. Mum, you look like a blushing bride!"

The music mellowed, and Mbuya and Sekuru meandered across the room, greeting their guests slowly returning to their seats. Hunger was getting the better of them, and Mwadiwa approached the podium with a microphone.

"Ladies and gentlemen, comrades, and friends!"

"Uncle Mwadiwa! We are not at a political rally!" That one exclamation above the din caused the crowd to burst into laughter.

"All right, no comrades then."

"Get on with it. Some of us have been on a bus all day!"

"Yes, I'm sure you're all starving, so you can move things along by not interrupting your MC… And by taking your seats quietly." Mwadiwa paused for people to settle down. Yet they kept talking.

"Everyone! I know you haven't seen each other for a long time. Not since Tawanda's funeral." There was a notable drop in the volume as Mwadiwa continued, "We are not here to mourn the aftermath of a shake-shake beer brawl." Sekuru's older sister shot Mwadiwa a piercing glare at the irreverence, but he stayed unabated, "Parents, grandparents, uncle and aunt, our special couple is everything to everyone. Today is Mbuya and Sekuru's 60th anniversary! It's now time for speeches. Who will break the ice? Uncle Desmond, please be brief. We don't have time for one of your meandering sermons!"

Uncle Desmond, Mbuya's eldest brother, walked to the podium, straightening his tartan bowtie and the grey suit jacket worn on such important occasions.

"Welcome, everyone, and thank you all for coming. No sermons today, I promise." He eyed a few family members pointedly, "But you should come and hear one some time. It might do you some good. I first met Sekuru, my brother-in-law, in the first form at St Francis Xavier School. I remember when he started courting my sister, this skinny fellow with scuffed shoes and not much to look at." He glanced mischievously at Sekuru, his beloved brother-in-law. "And not much has changed," he said with a crooked smile. "He was a good student, hard-working and undeniably bright. Smart enough to recognise a good future wife. But he was also dirt-poor. Mbuya pleaded with our parents to not charge him too much dowry when the time came. In the end, they let him off easy. I think everyone would agree it was a good decision. And look where they are now! I am sure I speak for everyone when I say that we are all so proud of you both for making it to 60 years."

Uncle Desmond narrated how the happy couple had succeeded in life through hard work, perseverance, love, and respect for each other. As successful entrepreneurs, they owned a fleet of luxury buses that travelled cross-border to South Africa and carried freight in the subregion as a side-line. Sekuru was unlike some of his contemporaries, whose heads were turned by wealth and the more money they accrued, the more pseudo-wives and concubines they accumulated. Mbuya and Sekuru were still together with two unspoilt children who had studied abroad and returned to their motherland.

Waiters began to move back and forth, serving hungry guests who had little time for protocol around speech giving. Unperturbed by cutlery noises, Uncle Desmond explained that although the couple were now grey-haired and nearing retirement, they had invested in a large residential property in the northern suburbs. What a success story to emulate! Turning to his two nephews, Mwadiwa and Simba, Uncle Desmond continued, "Thank you very much for arranging such a wonderful feast in this five-star hotel. Some of us could have died before entering such an attractive environment."

As Uncle Desmond sipped his red wine, Mwadiwa seized the opportunity to interrupt since it was now clear the alcohol was speaking. After eating dessert, the guests fidgeted, while some went for seconds at the buffet table. Others were now lounging in their chairs like beached whales. Grandchildren were chasing each other among the tables, a recipe for disaster.

"Thank you, Uncle Desmond, for that comprehensive overview," said Mwadiwa.

"But I haven't tol-."

"Thank you. You can take your seat. Have some dinner before Uncle Moses eats it all."

Sekuru was ready with his speech when Mwadiwa escorted the couple onto the podium and adjusted the microphone.

"Ladies and gentlemen, relatives and friends," Sekuru began. He squinted in the spotlight, wiped his brow, and loosened his tie. "I am not sure where to start." He continued, "You won't mind if I sit down. I'm not as young as I used to be. Mwadiwa, my son, help me with this microphone."

There were murmurings until Sekuru resumed in an emotion-filled voice, "When Mwadiwa came to fetch us this afternoon, we thought we were going to his house and lo and behold, here we are. We are both very pleased that this evening's celebration is ending in your company. It's like our wedding reception all over again, except we would never have been able to afford all this splendour. I know you all want to hear how we survived 60 years of marriage. I met my wife at secondary school, as Uncle Desmond mentioned. I first saw her when she watched football matches against rival schools in our league. Both Uncle Desmond and I were strikers in our heydays when we were quick and agile. I noticed her, a pretty girl among her friends, cheering on the sidelines. Desmond encouraged our courtship because I was initially afraid to date my best friend's sister. When he commented that I appeared interested, I said, 'Funny; I never really noticed her before!'" Laughter erupted in the room as Mbuya tried to conceal her embarrassment.

Sekuru continued, "There were no cell phones, and we didn't use telephones willy nilly. We also didn't have the pocket money for transport when Mbuya went to college. So, our relationship was on a slow burner for years. We stole chances to be together during the holidays. I'd visit Mbuya under the guise of spending time with Desmond. I'm sure initially he wasn't convinced I had honourable intentions. One thing led to another, and as Desmond told you, I decided to marry the love of my life. I had enough dowry for the customary first instalment. Mbuya has helped me pay off her dowry over the years. It has been a lifetime of hire purchase!" There were nodding heads among the male guests while some vocal women remonstrated in hushed voices that they were not goods to be bought and sold.

Sekuru continued, "I can now share this story because there are no consequences at my age. By the time her parents passed away, God rest their souls; we could even afford to take them to various resorts abroad. Back to our story. We had a simple wedding, and we meant it when we said our vows. 'Till death do us part.' We meant them. My wife and I have come a long way and don't think it was a leisurely ride! I'm sure you remember that Mbuya and I lost a child when we were still newly married. That was devastating. Then we lost my parents, who never enjoyed the fruits of our businesses. I regret not seeing the pride in my father's eyes. There were times when we also had disagreements, Mbuya and I. But we never spent more than a day before we made up. Mbuya has always been the steady hand both in the home and business. She worked as the accountant, and whatever profits we made, we planned our spending together. Not like the youngsters these days with separate bank accounts and talk of 'my money.' It was always our money. We planned things together, didn't we, Mbuya? We were careful not to allow people to get between us, not even our children. That's one of the causes of failing marriages. Sometimes grief comes not from friends but from evil vices such as spending one's life in the mists of alcohol and drugs. I am not saying I have no vices myself, but we should do everything in moderation."

Mwadiwa approached the podium, trying to catch his father's eye. Sekuru, now re-energised, said, "I can spend all evening talking about Mbuya and how she has been the woman behind the man, the mother to our children."

Sekuru wiped his brow and eyes with his handkerchief, and the room became silent. Trying to control his raw emotions, he continued, "This woman beside me has been my best friend since I first met her. She has put up with a lot. Every family occasion, whether births, weddings, or funerals, she has been the number one daughter in law; organised, efficient, and loving all in one. I could not have made a better choice of a lifelong companion."

Sekuru paused and slowly turned to his wife, dutifully still standing next to him; he took her hands and folded her in a loving hug. The crowd started to shout, whistle, and make a din in celebration. Sekuru's friends approached, shook his hand, and embraced him. They respectfully shook Mbuya's outstretched hand, and their wives came to join them with everyone ululating and dancing. There was an overwhelming outpouring of sentiment as the couple returned to their table.

Mwadiwa, now back in control, turned to his mother, "Mum, are you also going to make a speech? It's your day! A few words? I take it the shaking of the head means No. Okay. Now that your champagne glasses are full, let's toast to the wonderful couple. To my parents, your Sekuru and Mbuya, thank you so much for sharing your love story of 60 years! We wish that many of us could last that long in marriage."

The dance floor came alive as the music returned. Some guests became engrossed in exchanging anecdotal stories about how youngsters are getting married and divorcing, even within a year. Others said, "What we heard today is a wonderful story of true love and commitment!"

Mwadiwa again called the room to order and added a few sentiments to conclude the speeches. "My brother and I are witnesses to our parents' love and a result of this happy couple. We've never heard our parents quarrel, well, not in front of us, and they always remind us about the need to love one another and do good! Congratulations once again, and if we could, we would not have chosen better parents!"

The evening wore on as the DJ played rhumba and a myriad of local artists for the younger crowd. People made requests for their chosen songs of yesteryear. The anniversary couple took to the dance floor for a couple of their favourite numbers. They continued mingling among their guests, celebrating their life together, anticipating a few more decades until death parted them.

Memories from Childhood

It had been twenty-four years since Kurai had last seen the compound. The place looked, in essence, the same. Her grandparents' rural homestead was still intact, and the cluster of three-pole and mud huts had survived the test of time. Kurai's reminiscing was drawn towards the heart of the smallholding, a circular kitchen with its thatched roof, black with soot where the smoke from the wood fire had swirled upwards, escaping from the open hearth. Opposite were square-shaped sleeping quarters attached to a sitting room, all under a corrugated iron roof held down by old tyres and logs. The two small granaries perched on the granite crop were still precariously leaning as if they could slide, one day, down the slope into ruins. This was the place Kurai remembered as a child, staying under the watchful eye of her grandparents before re-joining her siblings in the city.

Whilst everything looked the same, the heart and soul of the place had long since gone. She didn't attend her grandparents' funerals, tragically one after the other, and the memory still vexed her soul. Kurai had called this her home, albeit for two years. It was now occupied by tenant farmers who had no history there.

Once overseas, Kurai couldn't or hadn't come back, even when her family wrote and told her that her grandparents were deteriorating. After joining a prestigious university, her studies became her excuse. It was a significant achievement, the first grandchild to study abroad.

Yet, she still recalled one conversation with her mother, "Kurai, you haven't rung us for some time, especially after telling you that your grandparents aren't well. They are asking after you."

"I thought I called you last week, and I must have lost track of time, what with upcoming exams."

"They don't know that! As their favourite grandchild, they are expecting you to arrive any minute. The rate they are deteriorating is worrying, and it's as if one cannot live without the other."

"Mum, I hear you. What do you want me to do? Abandon my studies and my final exams, yet I'm nearly there?

Can't I come after I…"

"No one is pressuring you, Kurai; we just thought you should know they are declining in health. But you know best."

"Help me out, Mum. Please explain my situation and send them my love."

"I will continue to reassure them that you are thinking of them. But I'm not sure how long your grandparents will be around. If it's money for your flights, we can send it."

The grandparents passed away soon after. Kurai took part in their funeral service on Zoom, which was impersonal but better than nothing. She sometimes wondered what they would have made of her First-Class Honours degree in Psychology since they had barely seven years of primary education between them.

Eventually, Kurai decided she couldn't continue as a perpetual student after completing postgraduate work, supported by a prestigious scholarship. She had embarked on it partly for the status and to escape the pressures of looking for a job. Even her parents began to question when she would start earning an income. The small matter of not having a husband was never far away when all her married peers talked of mortgages and babies. Kurai put off all these expectations as long as she could and finally succumbed to pressure from her aunts, who wanted their brother's daughter married and with someone in her old age.

Kurai's marriage, which was not made in heaven, didn't survive the seven-year itch when they returned home. Her spouse and in-laws did not take long to decide that Kurai was too much to cope with; not traditional enough, too opinionated, a feminist, whatever that meant.

"I have to say I told you so!" said her Aunty Sharon over several commiseration meetings. "You were so strong headed from day one, Kurai, when you as good as told your mother-in-law that your career came first, and you had no plans for any children any time soon. This was to someone who prides herself on being a homemaker. Yes, you may well frown, but…"

"Aunty, when we were abroad, the man I married appeared enlightened. We shared responsibilities around the home, and we were equals. How was I to know his strong traditional background would re-emerge in marriage?"

"You honestly thought that he would forget his roots after selecting the son of a chief as a life partner!"

"As my confidante, you should have set me straight at the time."

"Don't make me laugh, Kurai! You said you were in LOVE, and you thought we wanted to ruin your life. You were never going to be a traditional African wife!"

After the breakup, Kurai considered staying with her parents but decided against it. Their house rules and regulations were many, including who could visit, when to eat and what to wear. It was as if she had never left home. Instead, she successfully threw herself into climbing the corporate ladder while savouring the freedom to live life on her terms.

Kurai's conscience kept telling her she would regret not making her peace, having not visited her grandparents' graves because of the aftermath of her marriage breakup. When she eventually made the journey, the old homestead transported her back to her childhood. She rediscovered the rusty skeleton of an old tractor covered in a veneer of dust and cobwebs. It had entertained Kurai for hours as a child, imagining herself ploughing fields before the rains. Everything was frozen in time except that the grandparents were now just memories. This trip, however, had been a must. She needed to pay her respects and visit their last resting place, a makeshift communal graveyard near an anthill, beyond a gum tree plantation.

Kurai could not claim to have had a difficult childhood. Soon after marriage, her father left her mother with his extended family to study in South Africa. He came back occasionally to check on his fledgeling family. His wife soon discovered that motherhood was not a task taken lightly, even though her in-laws were concerned. Way back then, there were no qualms about sending young children to live with close relatives. So, when Kurai went to stay with her grandparents, the expectations were that she could cope with the separation from her parents during her formative years with no adverse psychological effects. In hindsight, she realised she had been sent there to relieve the childcare pressure on her parents and make way for her unborn siblings. Luckily, her grandparents longed to have a grandchild around, and two mangy guard dogs surviving on scraps of leftover food were her best friends.

As Kurai wandered around the homestead, she recalled that peasant farmers like her grandparents followed a seasonal ritual before the rains, heading daily to their plots, with food and drinking water. Through the day's scorching heat, no one was idle as they broke their backs preparing the fields for planting. Each evening, the family would trudge home, exhausted with their hoes over their shoulders, the women balancing precariously on their heads empty metal *kango* food containers and firewood. The whole country would then wait for darkening skies to herald the coming rainy season, its thunder clouds and lightning splitting the rain-laden skies.

With no one to play with, Kurai accompanied the adults daily, initially wanting to help them with her child-size hoe. When bored, she would sit under a shady tree, playing make-believe games with invisible friends and her old corn cob doll clothed in a rag dress.

Tired of entertaining herself one day in the unrelenting November sun, she pleaded to return home and play in the verandah, where the cold cement floor was a welcome relief from the ruthless heat.

"There is no one at home. Why can't you sit and play like you usually do under the tree? Do you want a drink of water?" said Grandmother.

"No. I want to go home."

"Who will look after you? You can't wander around on your own. Bad people may be roaming about, waiting to snatch unsuspecting children."

With the stubbornness and innocence of a child, Kurai set off home, saying, "I am not afraid. I can run very fast, scream, and you and the dogs will come and rescue me."

Kurai followed the narrow well-worn path, past a woodlot of tall eucalyptus, past the orchard full of citrus and peach trees. The homestead was eerily quiet. Under the veranda's cold, rusty corrugated iron sheets, Kurai became engrossed in her games. A deep guttural noise broke her solace, an inhuman sound coming from a rocky outcrop overlooking the homestead. A shadowy figure concealed in sackcloth suddenly appeared. Kurai could recall her piercing screams as she sped off at break-neck speed, in complete hysteria. In between tears while hiding herself in her grandmother's skirt, Kurai blurted out something about a *binya* (monster) that tried to capture her.

From that day, she stayed in the fields with everyone else. That childhood experience never left her subconscious. When older, she was told the bogeyman was her grandfather, who had played the prank on her.

Now back at the homestead, Kurai realised why it had taken her so long to return to where she had spent her formative years. Her childhood fears, a fabric of the place, were now buried with her grandparents in their unmarked graves. Kurai's mixed memories had kept the tenuous link with the homestead alive, which was all that mattered.

Another Shot At life

"Dad, you can't go on like this. The house is like a pit whenever I visit," said Tadiwa as she moved around the kitchen. "When did you last clean out the fridge? It's full of takeaways from heaven knows when and you're growing mould in here! There is enough dirty linen scattered around the house to keep a laundry firm in business. You also look as if you are sleeping in your clothes. Mum isn't coming back, and the sooner you internalise that fact, the better!"

Kundai had had enough after yet another tirade from his daughter Tadiwa. All the self-pity was threatening to drown him, yet he couldn't get out of the mire. His wife had left him some time ago, and his two adult children occasionally dropped in, probably more concerned about the family dog's welfare than their father. Tadiwa and her brother Simba never took sides in the arguments before or since the separation, and they were mature enough to know that there would be no winners. Kundai still couldn't understand how he had arrived in his current state, constantly licking his wounds with no end in sight. As a husband, he had been the classic textbook example of a dutiful provider all his married life. Ruby had walked out after their twenty-third wedding anniversary, her bottled-up anger exploding and smothering everyone in despair.

"If you subject me to verbal diarrhoea every time you come and visit, don't bother to come, Tadiwa!"

"I'm not picking a fight! I can't speak for Mum, but Simba and I care about you. You seem to be experiencing low-level depression. Are you sure you don't want to talk to someone?"

"The soon-to-graduate psychiatrist! Are you already diagnosing patients? I don't know why you two focus on me as a charity case. Leave me be, Tadiwa."

"You need to take your mind off things, Dad. Do you even have a social life? Why not join one of those dating sites and meet new people?"

"Have you and your brother Simba been talking about anything besides me? I don't need any of your help. I need a time out."

Exasperated, Tadiwa continued to move around the kitchen aimlessly.

"Okay, Dad, let's be brutally honest," Tadiwa continued, "when did you last go out, even with your buddies?"

"It's not the same anymore. I always relied on your mum, especially when with other couples. Even the dullest people sounded exciting, and I neither have the skill nor energy to emulate her."

Father and daughter sat down around the kitchen table and stirred their tea. Tadiwa wondered whether she had not overdone it as she took furtive glances at her father, who looked despondent and lost in thought. After scrolling on her phone, Tadiwa said,

"We can look at one or two websites together. If you don't want to spend money, we can go for the freebies. Sounds cheap, but until you know what you are looking for, why spend anything? Have you tried any of them?"

"No. Sounds like too much work," said Kundai staring into his now lukewarm tea.

"There are several for your age bracket. Let's see what sort of information the websites want. Here's one."

As Tadiwa scanned through the requirements, Kundai said, "Why do I feel I am being bulldozed into deciding to go along with this hair brain idea? I know you are concerned about me, and I love you for it. So, to get you off my back, I'll go along with you."

"There you go!" said Tadiwa with relief. "I'll read the reviews before splashing your name all over the internet. If there's any information you don't want to share, we can always skip it or explore another site. You should at least start on one of these applications."

Within a few weeks, Kundai increased his activity on the site Tadiwa had persuaded him to sign up and discovered it was not as dead as the reviews had indicated. After holding off parting with a membership fee, he finally decided to pay the $70 a month and make the most of what was offered. All the added benefits began to flood his inbox. Even though he had shaved off two years on his profile age and listed hobbies he had abandoned, several matches came up, and he went out with three people.

The first encounter didn't last long. It never really happened. Kurai arrived at the agreed venue and sat at a bar after ordering a small gin and tonic. His prospective date had chosen a meeting place, which rapidly filled up with after-work crowds half his age. He wondered, on second thoughts, about the wisdom of meeting up with a total stranger in unfamiliar territory. He couldn't even remember the persona he had created for himself online. Emptying his glass in three gulps, he paid and left.

The phone rang as Kurai changed into his nightwear.

"Hi Dad, how did it go?"

"It didn't."

"What do you mean it didn't?"

"I stayed for a short time, drank my G&T and came home. Online dating is not for me."

"I admit it's a bit intimidating. However, you probably left some poor soul at a table in your impatience, waiting for you and feeling like a nana. Isn't that a bit insensitive? Imagine if you had been left high and dry, we'd never hear the last of it. It's just nerves, Dad," said Tadiwa. "You said there had been lots of interest in your profile. So, try again. This time, let's not give up before you even start."

Tadiwa held back for a month, thinking she was part of the problem. However, her father's silence became unbearable, and curiosity got the better of her. One evening, she turned up unannounced and invited herself to dinner. It didn't take long for her to realise a transformation had taken place in her absence. The house was unrecognisable.

"Is there something I should know?" said Tadiwa throwing herself onto a sofa.

"No, not that I'm aware of. Why do you ask?"

"Well, something has happened. Have the dating sites been keeping you busy? It looks as if you are already entertaining visitors. You've spruced up the place. The trendy haircut and clean clothes!"

"After three disasters, I went back to my profile, and it wasn't the real me. You were right, life's too short, so I fixed it. I've been on a few dates since, and things are much better."

"Cut out all the backstory stuff, Dad. The suspense is killing me. When do I get to meet the lucky woman?"

"His name is Kuda."

Upside-Down Tree

'Upside-down tree' - that's me. The village children call me that because of the way I look when my leaves have fallen in the autumn. The villagers think I look strange, and some say I grew here in the centre of their compound by magic, but my seed was carried to this part of Africa by animals. I have relatives in Madagascar and even as far away as Australia. A story is sure to rise about us wherever a baobab grows, and I heard a tale of one in Zimbabwe whose hollow trunk can shelter 40 people.

I have cared for this village in all seasons for as long as I can remember, a very long time by their short reckoning. They should know that the baobab is their source of life. The Togolese people know we are sacred trees. They have a proverb, 'Wisdom is like a baobab tree: no one individual can embrace it.'

It doesn't matter to me what they think. I have a special place for Mbuya Nyatsuro, my custodian. She respects me while mainly keeping to herself. Mbuya is the old widow whose lean-to hut rests precariously against my broad trunk.

As the seasons come and go, hot, cold, then dry, Mbuya and I have survived the elements, despite diseases and bush fires. We share memories of a year when there was drought as far as the eye could see. Dust and whirlwinds blew across the barren fields whose fine soil formed like dunes. Dry maize stalks whistled in the wind as the dust spun grains of sand across the desolate landscape. I became everyone's best friend. The children would beg Mbuya to collect my monkey seeds in the pods, which had taken 15 or even 20 years to grow. They would crush them open and suck the tartness from the fruit. The mothers would use the pulp to make juice and fermented beer. Market women dug up my roots to make red dye, and my bark was woven into baskets and ropes for sale. Even the old medicine men who refuse to share recipes of their secret concoctions profited from my medicinal properties, stripping my branches, and boiling my leaves like spinach to cure illnesses.

One day, journalists with a film crew wrote a story about me. I eavesdropped as villagers watched the city folk in amazement and sought my shade while remarking that these interlopers had not done their homework about rural life. What of the woman who gave birth to triplets? And the son who studied overseas, supporting his old school every year, with gifts for star pupils? Or the master farmer's pumpkin winning awards at the local agriculture show? Surely these stories were more important than some yarn about an old tree that had been among them since time immemorial?

Despite the comments, the film crew said their audiences were far more fascinated by an old baobab tree they claimed could be over 2000 years old and an endangered species. The TV crew interviewed excited local children and their school science teacher, who explained that I was the centre of life and an essential source of food, water and shelter for wild monkeys, birds and even lizards. The children learned in the classroom that environmental tragedies could befall our communities if people continued their reckless land clearing, chopping down trees willy nilly. But their parents took little notice of them, saying children should be seen and not heard.

Most villagers knew they would never see themselves on-screen because only one television existed in a popular local bottle store. Children are only allowed to watch through the window because there is usually standing room only, especially during the European Football League season.

Although Mbuya was in her best clothes that day as they filmed, no one gave her five minutes of fame. Yet, she knew me better than anyone. She knew that at night when I was in bloom, colonies of bats would roost among my branches, feasting on the nectar-filled flowers. She had seen, on rare occasions, passing herds of elephants surprise the villagers and cause panic and consternation as the giants of the forest rubbed themselves against my trunk or tore my bark in search of water.

Sometimes Mbuya sweeps beneath my shade, an ideal place for meetings. The village court, chief and other clan members assemble at least once a month under my branches. Mbuya always knows when because children scurry back and forth on the appointed day carrying wooden benches from the nearby classrooms and arranging them in crescent shapes around three oversized tattered chairs where the '*dare*' takes place. No one would have thought there was much happening in the community. But when I hear the court cases, I sometimes wonder whether there are more criminals than law-abiding people.

One day, the court assembled under my canopy. Women sat on reed mats covering their heads with scarves while men perched on wooden benches in the shade. Some youngsters even climbed my branches to get a better view. Mbuya joined the crowd but sat at a distance, a respected and trusted community member.

During the court session, people came to the chief with complaints about their neighbours' cows wandering into vegetable gardens, a stolen bicycle, and a man who had beaten his wife after returning from a beer hall. The crimes were numerous, and the punishments punitive. I heard all their secrets and judgements, and even I would have gone as grey as the wise old chief, trying to keep the peace.

I am still standing tall and strong, propping up Mbuya's hut. But I recently heard disturbing stories from neighbouring villages, carried by the wind, and things do not bode well for my future and others like me.

Somewhere across the seas, people have found out that my fruit can be ground into powder, described as 'raw, whole food.' You may think that is a good omen, but I foresee mass production and packaging of my fruit for supermarkets as people increasingly appreciate my non-GMO organic qualities. I have visions of trucks and lorries coming to collect my seeds in bulk, stripping me bare and not even leaving any for Mbuya, the villagers and animals that rely on me. Rumours abound about some villagers who are part of the plundering, stripping us bare of our pods to sell to go-betweens in bustling city markets. All, so they can buy new TVs and watch the sports channels and nature documentaries like the one made in our village.

The future sounds very bleak. I know people say you cannot keep a good thing down, but I can see myself no longer the revered tree of life, the heart of communities. I may even become extinct. Yet all I want is to live another thousand years in my village among the animals and my people.

A Wicked Sense of Humour

Nadia knew Eric, her son, could not be trusted to spend April Fool's Day without coming up with some prank. With his wicked sense of humour, Eric was a man-child who never tired of practical jokes. That's how he was. Eric struggled to make friends, an only child growing up in a sheltered environment. In his loneliness, he treated his mother as the best toy ever.

Nadia was looking forward to a weekend away after the tedium of on and off lockdowns. She loved scenic drives into the country, visiting historic buildings and reminiscing about yesteryear when people had servants galore. Eric worked for the National Coach Service and organised outings nationwide for a disparate group of senior citizens every year as part of the NCS's social responsibility. This year, Eric had decided to accompany his mother on the annual treat.

After an hour's drive, the coach arrived at an imposing brick building resembling a castle on the outskirts of a small coastal town. Described online as a haven for senior citizens, most facilities were within walking distance from the town centre.

The last few weeks had been tense as Nadia thought about her future after retirement. She had become increasingly cranky, and her arthritis was now a recurring conversation piece. She wondered whether she was holding Eric back since he had talked of travelling—seeing the world before settling down. As they entered the pleasant seaside town, Nadia came out of her short snooze.

"I thought you said we are going for a break by the sea. Why are we heading down a lane directing us to Everglades Aged Care Home?"

"Mum, keep your hair on! This place has one of the best spars and accommodation for rent. People come here for retreats in their reasonably priced, self-contained, two-bedroom units with separate bathrooms and wonderful sea views. I found out that this place has a massive discount on its retreat facilities."

Nadia became increasingly unsettled as Eric continued, "While we are here, let's take a tour. It will be fun! Think of the fresh sea air! I hear there are wonderful walks along the beach and coffee shops galore in the town centre. There's even a butterfly museum nearby, and I knew you would like that."

As they approached the majestic entrance, the main door opened, and a bubbly-looking woman exuding authority and order in a multicoloured ensemble greeted them with a smile.

"Hello, Mr Dixon. Is this your mother? Welcome! You are just in time for a quick tour before we serve tea. My name is Tashaya, the administrator at Everglades. We spoke on the phone."

Perplexed, Nadia looked at Eric, who squeezed her hand and followed Tashaya. They entered a large foyer with an imposing vase of proteas displayed on a centre table. Tashaya ushered the remaining coach passengers down a narrow corridor with a slight whiff of detergent. At the end of the passage was a room occupied by a few older people in various states of wakefulness, each with a caregiver trying to cajole the residents into completing a puzzle or joining in a game. Some were seated in front of a muted TV in a smaller room, while others listened to soft classical music, staring vacantly into space. Through the French windows, Nadia could see a beautifully manicured garden with wicker chairs scattered around the patio and green lawns where residents were sitting in clusters. One or two were engrossed in an art class, while others ambled around the herbaceous borders.

"What are we doing here, Eric? Do we know anyone here? I don't want to be with these people! They make me feel old and decrepit," said Nadia. "Is there a point to all this?"

"Let's have a look around. A life without any responsibilities, imagine that!" said Eric.

"Where will you be while I'm enjoying your idea of an idyllic life? Is this yet another attempt to put me in a home against my wishes?"

"Come this way," said Eric as he opened double doors into a sizeable unoccupied room decorated with party regalia and laid out for high tea.

Eric shouted, "Surprise and Happy Birthday!" as he switched on the lights. The adjacent doors opened, and Nadia's friends streamed in, hugging her and congratulating Eric on keeping the secret. Smiling, Tashaya slipped out quietly. Nadia was overwhelmed as familiar faces eventually sat around tables laden with food.

"Eric, please help me to a chair. The excitement is getting to me!"

"Mum, are you OK? Don't you like the surprise party?"

"I am very grateful that you organised a celebration for me. But find me a seat and open the windows. I am getting chest pain and nausea. Please don't make a fuss! I know everyone has tried to be here."

Sitting by the window, fanning herself and appearing to recover while sipping a glass of water, Nadia said, "This is an odd place to have a party. Is this your idea of an April Fool's Day joke?"

Eric, however, looked concerned and left the room as the guests discussed the situation in hushed, anxious tones.

"What's wrong with you, Birthday Girl?" said Mavis, Nadia's boisterous best friend. "You look a bit peaky on such a happy occasion. It's not often people of our age turn 70 years."

"Mavis, I'm so glad you're here. Please tell me you didn't know that Eric was bringing me here for my birthday. You know how I feel about these places. Did you see all those miserable souls on our way in? It makes me shiver to think about it. Even the sign out front gave me heart palpitations."

"Nadia, please try to calm down. Your breathing is getting laboured, and you don't sound like your usual self. Where has Eric gone?"

"I don't know," said Nadia. "Where is that child when you need him? Oh! Here he comes."

Nadia reached out to Eric, accompanied by a semi bald, middle-aged man walking with a surprising spring in his step. He was dressed in a brown tweed suit, a white shirt, and a bow tie. He had an engaging smile that roused Nadia out of her light-headedness. Eric knelt next to his mother's chair, holding her hand tentatively as he tried to gauge her mood.

"I am Dr Sims, and I have a resident patient here. However, Eric says you need medical attention? What seems to be the problem?" Dr Sims swiftly proceeded to start a physical examination of Nadia.

"I don't know what came over me," she replied.

The partygoers continued glancing in Nadia's direction, and conversations gave way to hushed comments about events in the corner where she was sitting. Dr Sims turned to Tashaya, "Is there another room with some privacy? I want to conduct a couple of basic tests."

Dr Sims asked follow-up questions and continued his examination based on Nadia's reported symptoms.

"I can't determine a diagnosis without a more thorough examination. You say you are feeling extreme fatigue and a sense of the room closing in on you?"

Eric butted in, "She was fine when we left home! I don't understand how all this started. This isn't how I planned the party weekend. We have a room full of guests and…"

"Based on my diagnosis, Eric, the planned party is the least of your worries," said Doctor Sims. "Nadia, I have conducted an initial examination, and given the symptoms you described, I am calling an ambulance immediately. I suspect a mild heart attack. Tashaya, please assist by calling 000, and the paramedics can take over."

Increasingly distraught and clutching Eric's hand, Nadia said, "You will come with me in the ambulance?"

Later that afternoon, Eric stood nervously by his mother's hospital bed, "Mum, how are you feeling now?"

"I must have fallen asleep, probably the effects of the medication. I recall vaguely Dr Sims, or was it another doctor, telling me about a suspected heart attack?"

"Mum, there is nothing 'suspected' about it. You are in the capable hands of Dr Taylor, the hospital's heart specialist, and he says you are fortunate that Dr Sims acted so quickly. You've been moved into a private room and need rest," said

Eric. "Dr Taylor is doing his rounds and will pop in again before leaving if you have any questions."

"Don't look so worried, Eric."

"I didn't know that the symptoms of a heart attack are so simple. I should've taken you more seriously when you mentioned discomfort in your upper back, the shortness of breath and pain in your left arm. You have always appeared invincible. You gave us all quite a scare!"

"You're not the only one," said Nadia, looking drained while smoothing her bedsheets.

Eric said, "Was it the surprise party that triggered all this?"

"I'm as confused as you are. By the way, I hope you've apologised to our guests, and I assume they have dispersed already?"

"Your friends, as planned, checked into the holiday units behind the aged care home. They send their good wishes. However, don't change the subject, Mum! If there is something you're worried about, please tell me. We don't want a repeat performance."

"Everglades Aged Care Home! Were you going to leave me there – even after I told you so many times that I don't want to stay in an aged care facility?"

"I heard you, Mum, when you said you would rather stay home. But in the long run, is it practical? Especially if I move out? After a short stay at the facility, you may yet change your mind."

"So, you organised the trip under false pretences and piggybacked on the National Coach Service's outing?"

"It was a rather insensitive reasoning in the light of day. I'm sorry, Mum."

"The 'insensitive reasoning', as you call it, could have gone badly wrong. I hope you can now respect my retirement wishes, and it's just as well I had packed a weekend suitcase."

Nadia, sounding more reconciliatory, said, "I'll still hold you to your promise of taking me away for a few days once I'm discharged. I deserve a break after my scare. Now shoo Eric and leave me to get some rest."

Smoke and Mirrors

The landline rang early when Baba and Mai were still eating breakfast. By the time they picked the receiver up, it had stopped. Then Baba's cell phone started buzzing incessantly.

"Who is it with no respect for public holidays? We've only just woken up. It's Easter Monday, for goodness sake!" said Baba.

"Baba, answer it!" Mai was growing impatient. "The landline never rings unless there's an emergency."

"Hello. Oh, it's you, Jess. What's wrong? Are you OK? What? When?" Baba moved to a chair and sat down. Mai drew nearer.

"Is it Jess? What's she saying, Baba?"

Baba gestured for quiet, "But we talked to you both yesterday! He never mentioned a thing. Really? That's terrible. Do you want me to come over? Okay, we're still eating breakfast. I'll tell your mum, and she can lay extra places for you and the children. I am so sorry, Jess. Let's talk when you get here. Drive safely."

"What's wrong?" Mai repeated, her eyes wide, "Is everyone okay? Is Jess coming with Bvunzai?"

"No. Only Jess and the children. I couldn't make head or tail of what she was saying. Something about Bvunzai getting arrested early this morning and the police arriving with a search warrant and turning their house upside down. They took his computer, two laptops, and Bvunzai's papers. Jess is now leaving the police station, although she couldn't talk to Bvunzai, only his lawyer."

"This can't be happening. Are the children okay?"

"They are fine, thank God. Can you believe it! Bvunzai - incarcerated! Let's wait till Jess arrives to tell us the whole story."

"That's awful! Did he say anything to you yesterday? I hope my poor grandchildren didn't witness the police searching their home. And poor Jess. Bvunzai is such a nice young man from a respectable family!"

Peering anxiously past the main door he had left ajar, Baba said to Mai, "You've always had a soft spot for our son in law. Jess has arrived. Go and meet her since you are better at consoling than I am."

Jess entered the house, looking dishevelled, red-eyed, and snivelling, trying to retrieve tissues from her bag while the children clung to her jeans. Mai escorted her in, an arm enveloping her daughter.

"Come in, come in. Oh, my poor baby! Let's move into the kitchen. The children can eat in the verandah while we talk. I'll put the kettle on. While you are drinking your tea, you can start from the beginning. Baba don't hover over her! Take a seat, Jess."

"Mum, it's all falling apart," said Jess as she narrated her story with broken sentences and sobs in between.

"Your dad and I are so sorry that you are being put through this trauma."

"I knew his lifestyle was too good to be true," Baba muttered.

"Speak up, Baba; we can't hear you. If you are going to contribute to the conversation, you must speak louder. What did you say?"

"Nothing, Mai. Nothing. Let Jess finish."

Sipping herbal tea, Jess became calmer, and Mai said with a nervous smile, "What an Easter! I can't believe this is happening to us. Baba had shared snippets from your call. It's worse than I thought."

"We haven't even been married for a year! I feel like I'm in a horrible nightmare," said Jess.

Baba, never good at handling emotional scenes, said, "Don't be so hard on yourself. You and the children should stay here till this mess is cleared up. So where is Bvunzai now? He should be here explaining himself."

"He's been in custody since this morning. I tried to get the facts from him, but he became evasive and kept saying he's been mistaken for someone else and would be out soon."

"Oh, my word!" said Mai, "You shouldn't have to go through all this by yourself. Baba, isn't there anything we can do?"

"Jess, have you contacted Mr Mhlunga, our family lawyer?"

"Our lawyer, Mr Mungati, arrived just before I left the police station. I spoke to him briefly in the corridor. He said he would talk to Bvunzai. I wasn't much use, what with a splitting headache. Mr Mungati assured me he would share as much as possible, barring lawyer/client privilege, and advised me to go home and rest. That's when I phoned you."

Mai interjected, "Jess, Jess, slow down. I'm trying to process what you are saying. I thought Bvunzai had been doing well at work. Didn't he recently get that big contract for the mining machinery?"

Baba kept quiet with a worried look. Jess said, "Mum, I am not sure I can tell you anything else. Driving here, I realised I know little about Bvunzai's business dealings."

The front doorbell rang just as they finished breakfast. Baba got up, muttering, "This is all we need!"

On the doorstep stood a man in his mid-40s, impeccably dressed in a handmade suit, crocodile shoes and matching briefcase, exuding the kind of confidence that came at a price.

"Good morning, my name is Alex Mungati of Tembo, Mhlunga, Mungati and Associates. Your daughter, Mrs Moyo, asked me to come. You must be Bvunzai's father-in-law. I believe you know one of our senior partners, Mr Mhlunga, and he's mentioned you play golf together."

Baba appeared surprised. "Come in, come in. Yes, I know Mr Mhlunga very well. You've already met my daughter, and this is my wife, Mavis. Jess, how did you manage to afford this guy?"

"Thank you for coming, Mr Mungati," Jess said, ignoring the question.

Mr Mungati briefed Baba, Mai, and Jess succinctly, despite the family's eagerness for minute details. He shielded any awkward questions as they bombarded him about Bvunzai's alleged crime. The little he shared was that the authorities had accused Bvunzai of being part of an international syndicate involving computer-based advance fee scams. After a multi-country investigation, Bvunzai had been identified as the alleged mastermind behind the siphoning of millions of dollars from unsuspecting individuals.

Mai said, "Mr Mungati, how can Bvunzai be involved? Our son in law?"

Baba ignored the interjection and asked, "Our son in law runs a legitimate business. Surely this is a case of mistaken identity?"

"All I can say, Baba and Mai, is the matter is still under investigation, but it is unlikely that your son in law will get bail. Many people are involved in the alleged crime," said Mr Mungati.

Mai said, "Baba, is this like what you were trying to explain to me last week about your spam mail? The one from a total stranger asking you to help transfer money?"

"Yes, Mai. The perpetrators are adept at disappearing online after the victims make payments."

Jess joined in, "I've heard of such cases, gullible individuals parting with their bank details resulting in money being siphoned from their accounts. But as for my Bvunzai being involved?"

Mr Mungati resumed, "Some people don't notice the small withdrawals till the bank questions the customer about suspicious transactions or the account holder discovers the fraud. It is simple and yet sophisticated and plays on people's greed."

Mai, still looking puzzled, said, "But if it is a few dollars here and there at the onset, how does it get into millions?"

Mr Mungati said, "Imagine if the scam is scaled up and you send the spam mail to millions of people across the globe. It's like fishing. Some get hooked, and others become wise and report to their banks."

"We've taken enough of your time Mr Mungati. You charge by the hour, and as my father said, you are not exactly cheap! I'm sure you have other cases to attend to. Thank you very much for coming round and briefing us. Let me escort you out, and please keep us posted," said Jess.

Returning from the front door, Jess looked dejected. Mai brewed a new pot of tea, and everyone resumed their seat around the kitchen table.

"This is all becoming surreal. I can't believe Bvunzai could be involved in such criminality," said Jess.

"I don't know," Baba said pensively. His brief comment did not reassure Jess, wilting by the minute. She couldn't look him in the eye, afraid to further expose her lack of knowledge about the finances in her marriage. Baba turned to Jess and said, "Are you telling me you suspected nothing, yet you lived under the same roof?"

"Baba, you know I have never been very good with money," said Jess defensively. "I have little to do with his business deals. I just assumed he was doing well, and we could afford the expensive holidays, the children's private school fees and living in one of the most expensive suburbs in the city."

Baba said, "But surely, my dear, you discuss finances in your marriage?"

"When I was inquisitive early in our courtship, he would fob me off and talk about investing well or winning massive contracts. His mantra was I shouldn't worry; he would provide. Who doesn't want a comfortable life? Remember when I married him, he promised I'd never have to work again, and I allowed myself to believe him."

"Pity. I don't know much about the industry Bvunzai operates in," said Baba. "I'm sorry, Jess. I hope for your sake that everything is legitimate."

Jess said, "Baba, you've had reservations about Bvunzai, yet you didn't talk to me about them? This is my husband we are talking about, the father of your grandchildren!"

"My dear. It's not a comfortable conversation, and you are also not the easiest person to talk to at times."

"Oh, so it's now all my fault?"

"You two, lower your voices. My poor grandchildren will hear every word." Mai turned to Jess, "Bvunzai is innocent until proven guilty. However, I can't also help thinking about your expensive wedding, our European holidays, and our recent house refurbishment. Should we be worried?"

"Your guess is as good as mine. I hope and pray it's not true."

Baba mumbled, "If it is true, I don't know how we will live in this city when all this comes out in the open—having a son in law as a thief!"

"You're not reassuring at all, Baba and Mai. Bvunzai is part of our family, and you both gave us your blessing when we married."

Oblivious to Jess' comments, Baba continued, "I always thought he was a Jonny-come-lately. His flashy cars and foreign trips and whatever-you-want-I can-provide attitude."

"If my husband is a thief and God forbid, we have all enjoyed the spoils of his wealth," said Jess. "None of us ever questioned how Bvunzai financed the luxuries we enjoy, and at Christmas, we were even campaigning for the next family holiday in the Bahamas."

Jess re-joined the conversation after answering her phone, "I'm afraid there is more. That was Mr Mungati with an update. Bvunzai told me he was going for a business trip abroad this week."

"And…? Don't keep your mother and me in suspense!"

"Mr Mungati says two plane tickets found in the police raid were one way. One is for Bvunzai, and can you believe this? The other is under the name of Julia Saudi."

"You mean Julia, the one who lives with you?"

"Yes, Mum, the one who lives with us," said Jess. "Bvunzai introduced her as his cousin looking for a job."

"So, she's not related to him? And again, you didn't suspect anything?" said Baba in astonishment.

"I just assumed Bvunzai, and Julia were close. It happens. But can you believe they would have left the children and me high and dry? Good riddance to bad rubbish! At least I still have the house and cars." said Jess angrily.

Baba interrupted, "I wish life were that simple, my dear. How do we know that the house was not put up as collateral for Bvunzai's business and will not be seized? Even your two cars, the Range Rover, and the Lexus, which are still on hire purchase, there's no guarantee they will not be repossessed since everything is going pear-shaped. We should prepare for the worst, Jess dear. Bvunzai's local bank accounts are probably empty or will be frozen."

"But how will we live?" said Jess, dissolving into tears in her mother's arms.

"The court will probably give you a small living allowance for daily expenses until the true picture comes out," said Baba.

Mai looking forlorn, said, "We've heard enough for one day. It can't get any worse. Let's go and check on the children."

Baba entered his study, closed the door, and called Mr Mhlunga, his friend and golfing partner.

"Jeff, I want to thank your law firm for taking up my son in law's case. It sounds like a right mess. I didn't want to share my additional concerns with your Mr Mungati and my family at this stage. We are all distraught," said Baba. "Bvunzai asked me for a loan about six months ago to enter a mining venture. I took him at his word and agreed he could start re-paying in six months. I didn't do any credit checks since he's family. With what is happening, and if he is involved, will I get any of it back? It's not a small amount, about 500K. What do you think?"

Jeff replied, "My friend, you know I can't talk about your son in law's case. However, if the matter goes to court, the media will have a field day, and your daughter will need your support."

"One last question Jeff," said Baba, "What will happen to the workforce? One of Bvunzai's employees in sales is my nephew, and he is doing so well."

"Again, I can't respond on an ongoing case. My colleague will endeavour to do his best for all parties involved."

"What a mess! Let me get back to the family and try and calm the waters. Thank you once again for your support."

Appearing unperturbed, Baba joined the family. "Mai, Jess, what a day! The next few weeks are going to be rough. I can't help but wonder whether his mother knows about his criminal activities. You know how close they are."

"Baba, as you said earlier, we can only hope that it's a case of mistaken identity!" said Mai.

"Can the children and I stay here overnight? I don't think I can cope with all this drama. And I'm not even sure whether Bvunzai will be out soon," said Jess.

"By all means," said Baba, "I've no intention of visiting Bvunzai in detention, but your mother and I will support you if the case comes to trial."

Jess replied, "Mai and Baba, I am so sorry to involve you."

"Nonsense, this is not your fault," Mai said, wrapping an arm around her daughter and squeezing her shoulder.

"Baba, you have a right to say I told you so–"

"No, Honey, I would never–"

"But you had your doubts all along."

Sounding cryptic, Baba said, "Unfortunately, I'm good at dishing out advice, but I don't always listen to my sixth sense. Let's hope we'll survive this crisis."

Raw Wounds

Heidi arrived at the meeting feeling very self-conscious. She was experiencing second thoughts about whether it had been a clever idea to accept the invitation as the guest speaker at the Women in Action club meeting. Busi, the chairperson and an old school friend, was hard to refuse.

As Heidi entered the hall, she was pleasantly surprised by the turnout. The club room was jam-packed. People were still milling about with a few minutes to go, absorbed in small talk, and picking up refreshments. Latecomers were hunting for seats and swapping chairs to accommodate their bad backs. No one called anyone a hypochondriac, but there were enough of them claiming various ailments. There was a buzz in the room with usual suspects seeking sympathy over work and domestic situations.

"Ladies, ladies! Let's settle down. Our guest speaker is an extremely busy woman. We mustn't keep her waiting. I hope everyone has signed in," said Busi as she tried to bring some semblance of order. Busi, a stickler for time, continued, "We would like to welcome Dr Heidi Chiremba, a long-serving member who has returned from her leave of absence. She is our esteemed guest for International Women's Day. Dr Chiremba's medical practice is part of the Well Women's Clinic behind the Town Hall, for those of you who might not know. Her topic today is Spousal Abuse. I know there will be many follow-up questions. So, let's get started. Dr Chiremba, the floor is yours. You have 20 minutes, followed by a Q and A session."

Dr Chiremba had graduated at the top of her medical training class. She knew many community members looked up to her as a role model, particularly after she successfully championed the opening of the Women's Clinic. She had a matronly figure with a salt and pepper mop of wild curls. Her warm perpetual smile made patients feel the empathy oozing out of her every word. The motley crowd in the audience waited in anticipation as she prepared to deliver her address. The topic was broad, but she was adept at animated presentations.

"Thank you very much for allowing me to give this talk. I was a highly active club member, but lately, I have thrown all my energy into my day job at the clinic. Once I finish my talk, I am open to questions and please don't hesitate to contact me at the clinic for a private consultation."

There followed a laboured pause. Busi looked at Heidi, who filled the silence by re-adjusting the microphone and straightening her handwritten notes, a prop in her sweaty hands. She didn't need prompting, but her confidence levels had suffered over the past year. Why had she agreed to talk on such a sensitive topic, especially in a room full of familiar faces? It was now too late to back down. Busi placed a glass of water in front of Heidi and smiled in encouragement while squeezing her friend's hand surreptitiously.

Heidi refocused on her audience and continued, "Spousal Abuse can happen to the best of us. Each of us knows someone who has been impacted. It's no longer a dirty secret. You have already heard a lot about this year's International Women's Day theme, 'Women in Leadership: Achieving an Equal Future in a COVID-19 World.' I am tying the theme to spousal abuse because within our homes, not all our spouses promote and encourage us to take up leadership positions, especially those steeped in our patriarchal society. Abuse is a broad term taking many forms, including psychological, emotional, sexual, financial, and domestic violence. We all know that domestic abuse can happen to anyone. Like many of you, I have come to meetings like this where someone shared statistics on our patriarchal society and women's struggle in leadership roles while experiencing a lack of support or even direct opposition from within their own homes. Like many of you, I thought this was something that happened to someone else." Heidi took a sip. "I was a victim of domestic abuse, and I didn't even realise how far from okay my situation was. Today I'm going to talk about what happened to me and hope it will stimulate a lot of us in the room to re-examine our lives."

From her vantage point at the podium, she could sense discomfort among the audience, and she touched raw nerves as she outlined the abuse cycle and shared case studies. After a while, Busi scribbled a note and passed it to Heidi, who glanced at it and nodded.

Busi said, "Ladies, let's take a short break and then return to a question-and-answer session. Thank you very much, Heidi, for your address so far on such a pertinent topic."

Busi shielded her friend from the crowd and steered her towards a table laden with snacks where some club members stood in clusters, speaking in low voices while glancing at Heidi in curiosity.

After the short break, Heidi returned to the podium, and after touching on coping mechanisms and life choices, she concluded, "I should now like to open the floor to questions."

Several hands went up as Heidi, although beginning to wane, responded to questions about global statistics and why people do not report abuse or leave abusive spouses. Someone mentioned the issue of denial. However, a sense of fragility was now beginning to overwhelm her. With a sideward glance, she appealed to Busi for help. Busi signalled the end of the meeting, followed by a member delivering a vote of thanks.

Sitting afterwards in a nearby café over coffee, Busi clasped Heidi's hand, "Thank you so much for opening up to us. You did very well, Heidi. I can't believe you kept it together. Not many people can share firsthand experiences on such a sensitive topic without breaking down."

"I almost crumpled," said Heidi. "It has been getting easier to talk about my experiences, and I keep telling myself that it is therapeutic to share what happened. And good for others to hear it."

"A few in the audience looked quite uncomfortable when you shared Matthew's appalling behaviour towards you. It's conceivable that some who left early may have felt your experiences were too close to the bone."

"Maybe."

"Until you told me your disturbing story a month ago, I honestly didn't know what was happening in your life. I'm sorry I wasn't there for you."

Heidi sighed. "To tell you the truth, for a long time, I was more concerned about what you and my family would think. Matthew and I worked so hard to keep up the appearance of a successful couple living the life. Yet underneath all that, I dreaded going home."

"That must have been so horrible."

"It was my daily torment over the last year. Matthew constantly undermined me with his mind games. I resorted to throwing myself into my work as a coping mechanism. I'm just really grateful you gave me a place to stay when I finally left him."

"It's the least I could have done. Don't answer if you are not comfortable, Heidi. I never asked you when did it all start? Matthew was such a lovely social animal in the early days of your marriage, and who would have thought he was also a Jekyll and Hyde character underneath all that."

"I was blindsided! He initially was so subtle," said Heidi. "I sometimes think it may have been when I started my business and became the Well Woman Clinic Practice Manager. There was a lot of positive media publicity around our services. Matthew felt neglected and overshadowed because of my success. But he never verbalised it. I have always tried to do a balancing act and not neglect my responsibilities at home. However, as the business became profitable, Matthew became pricklier. He kept saying it was all a fluke, and people would soon figure out how clueless I was."

"He was jealous of your success?"

"Could be. It was around the time his company went bust. He

spent time at home and started asking me to account for every cent."

"You poor thing!"

"Do you remember when I kept cancelling meetups with you?"

"Don't I just!"

"He obsessed over whom I socialised with, including seeing my parents! Our social life ground to a halt. I only found out later that he had put a tracker on my phone and took to listening to my calls. I got to a point where I started calling friends from work, so I wouldn't have the third degree about what they wanted and how they were always in our business."

"I am so sorry, Heidi," said Busi. "When you said you wanted to have a break from attending our club meetings, I didn't know you were going through so much."

"It's not your fault. You are the only person we wanted to impress, so we were on our best behaviour whenever we met up with you. I honestly felt at some point that it was all my fault, and no one would believe what I was going through."

"What a nightmare!"

"It's been a long journey, Busi. Marriage counselling was a nonstarter because Matthew saw it as airing dirty linen in public. I eventually thought through the pros and cons and decided I needed to get out, at least for a while. He was never violent, so I suppose that at least was good, but he made me feel so inadequate. I couldn't cope. It was too much."

Busi nodded but said nothing.

"My doctor set me up with a psychiatrist, Bev. You met her, didn't you? She helped me understand that Matthew's ghosting and accusations were emotional abuse."

"You've done well to come through all this in one piece."

"Yes and no. I still feel fragile sometimes. It comes and goes. Outward appearances can be deceptive."

"Please don't beat yourself up, Heidi. Seeking help is not a sign of weakness."

"Thanks for letting me rant! There need to be more people with a sympathetic ear, like you."

"But look how long it took me to realise your situation, and I'm one of your closest friends."

"Making me talk at the club today is part of the healing process. I hope I didn't come across as too emotional and needy."

"No! No. I understand it'll take time. But you are one brave woman, having to cope with separation and loss of confidence in someone you loved. After such a powerful presentation today, Heidi, please re-consider renewing your club membership. You're an inspiration to us all."

Home Sweet Home

Lindiwe, back from doing overtime, hurriedly closed the front door of her lodging in anticipation of her sister's call. It had been snowing all night and would continue all day. Heading for her attic bedsit, she entered the communal kitchen. She looked in despair at the kitchen sink overflowing with dirty dishes before retrieving her mug, which someone had left unwashed. It was a recurring problem, and there was never anyone obvious to blame. She took her tea upstairs into her small cubbyhole, advertised as a reasonably priced single room with all amenities under one roof. The estate agent had deliberately not mentioned that there was not enough room to swing a cat, never mind keeping her possessions. Her meagre furniture consisted of a fold-away desk, a battered old chair with lumpy cushions and a wooden wardrobe with a warped mirror which made her look twice her size. Under her single bed, a battered suitcase full of discarded, too thin, or too colourful clothes she had bought second-hand in flea markets back home in Harare was gathering dust. Even her new shoes had turned out to be unsuitable, with no grip on London's slippery, icy streets.

While sipping her now lukewarm tea, Lindiwe perched on her bed. The surrounding snow-coated rooftops glistened against the backdrop of a clear blue sky. The communal garden was immediately below her window ledge, where occasionally, non-descript birds visited the now frozen birdbath near the sentry-like tall yew trees. She could hear the intermittent hum of distant traffic and an occasional 'ping' from her self-regulating radiator. The beautiful scenery did not detract from the depressing cold temperatures of her adopted country. In the 'Come to the UK to fill well-paid job vacancies and get a better life' brochures, there had been no mention that winter would go on forever, and the sun would only occasionally come out, playing hide and seek behind the clouds.

"Hello? Hello? I can't hear you. Oh, it's you, Maida. You sound so faint!"

"Sis Lindiwe? I am already shouting! How can you not hear me? I'll switch off the video."

"That's much better. How are you? It's such a relief to hear a familiar voice in my mother tongue. You know, spending one's days speaking and thinking in English is exhausting!" They both laughed.

"Seriously, Lindiwe, you sound low. What's wrong?"

"Nothing. I am tired after finishing my shift. Taking two trains every day to work is no joke, and it eventually takes its toll. I nearly missed my stop because I was already dozing off. I'm just drained these days."

"I keep telling you to slow down, Lindiwe, and you don't listen. We don't want you returning home with lots of health problems."

"I can't afford to move nearer work to reduce the commute. But I'm lucky my current employer allows me to work nights permanently in the care home, and it's the only way I can earn extra money. Our parents' new house is not going to build itself."

"Speaking of which, let me fill you in before my phone battery runs low," said Maida, "our electricity has gone, another outage. I won't be able to recharge before this evening."

"What's happening back home?" Lindiwe said in despair. "We never used to have all this constant load shedding."

"The power cuts are better now that they have shut down the industries because of the Covid-19 curfew. Once that's over, we are back to power rationing till the middle of the night. Then everyone gets up to charge phones, cook, hoover, iron. You name it! Night becomes day."

Lindiwe's response was barely audible, and Maida said, "Lindiwe, are you still there?"

"Yes, I said it's the same old story, Maida. We complain about our leaders, and then no one does anything. We circumvent the problems they create. That's what we're good at, complaining. We are political cowards; however, that's not why you phoned, is it?"

"Dad asked me to ask you to send a bit extra this month."

"What do you mean a 'bit extra'? Where am I supposed to get the 'bit extra' from?"

"Don't shoot the messenger!"

"OK. Sorry! How much extra and what for?"

"I told Dad you wouldn't be happy. I know you're sending as much as you can. But things are tight here."

"Where are things not tight, Maida? Do you know that I can barely pay my rent after sending money home? I don't think the parents realise how difficult and expensive it is, living in this country. The only decent meal I get is at work; otherwise, I live on junk food. I haven't bought any new clothes, and I'm lucky we wear uniforms for work. It's cold here, nothing like the winter at home. I get frostbite in my fingers and toes even in winter clothes."

"Lindiwe, Mum's in hospital."

"Oh, no! Since when? What's wrong with her?"

"She was admitted two nights ago. We didn't phone you because we knew you would panic, and we didn't want to disturb your sleep after your night shift."

"Poor Mum. Is it serious?"

"We don't know what's wrong, and she's had so many tests. I know that Dad was in a real state when he phoned me at work, and I just dropped everything and went home to take her to the emergency 24-hour clinic. She said she was feeling weak and having trouble breathing."

"That doesn't sound good. Why didn't Dad call an ambulance to take her to the public hospital?"

"You're so out of touch, Lindiwe. When did you last catch up on the news from home? The ambulance services are charging a lot! The nurses are still on strike in public hospitals, demanding more pay. Both the government and nurses' unions are stubborn, and their negotiations are going nowhere. If you want treatment, you must use the private hospitals and pay through the nose. Before they admit you, they want to know which medical cover you are on. Otherwise, it's cash up-front."

"I thought Dad's medical aid covered Mum?"

"She's covered, but he now has a shortfall. You remember she went to hospital with her kidney disease and then there were all the specialists. Dad's government pension can't stretch that far. I'm working extra hours, but I earn peanuts! We wouldn't ask you if we could cope, especially after you helped so much with Mum's dialysis. Tapiwa's school fees, our parents' daily maintenance and all the Covid funerals the parents have contributed to depleting our reserves. It's getting terrible here, and people are dropping like flies."

"The death rate is no better here, Maida, especially in the nursing homes. I only hope Mum and Dad are not exposing themselves at these numerous funerals; otherwise, they will catch the virus. No one seems to respect social distancing based on the TV snippets I've seen. People might as well go mask-less. Some are wearing them under their chins or with noses out; you name it!"

"I've tried warning Mum and Dad about Covid, and I even stopped driving them to the rural areas where the level of awareness is appalling. There is little else I can do. They keep saying if we don't bury our friends and relatives, who will mourn us? It's like they think there is an attendance register."

"Maybe not a physical one…" Lindiwe chimed in.

"Seriously," Maida added, 'there's continuous and subtle peer pressure, especially for Mum. Her church group keeps her abreast of what's happening, and she's now our news source regarding who has died, where, and of what. That's aside from coping with our own relatives' demands for financial support. So, she feels obliged to go."

"Can't Dad stop her?"

"You know our mother has a mind of her own! Since Dad's retirement, he has also joined her with most of his potentially vulnerable friends whose badges of success are being overweight and unfit! The only people benefitting from this pandemic are medical facilities and funeral parlours. Can you believe there are now specialised Covid-19 doctors who conduct house calls, charging exorbitant prices!"

"I'm sorry I snapped at you earlier, Maida. I got a bit wrapped up in my own stressing issues. If you weren't there, I don't know who'd look after Mum and Dad. I have work friends from other countries - we're all in the same predicament. We work ridiculous hours and do what we can. Things are tough everywhere. I'm getting paid tomorrow, so I'll send you some money by the quickest means, and please text me when it arrives. Sorry, I must rest before my next shift. Speak to you soon."

Trying to fight off the self-pity that had enveloped her, Lindiwe took down her photo album and flicked through fading pictures. Occasionally she would peek through her frosty bedroom window beyond the icicles hanging off the cornices and stare along the street where cars were making furrows in the newly fallen snow. People were walking purposefully along the pavement, heading for unknown destinations.

A week later, Lindiwe received another call, "Hi, Maida. It's unlike you to phone when I am supposed to be sleeping. What's up?"

'Hi, Sis. How's work?"

"Something's up. I can tell. Your timing has gone awry, Maida. I have only just got into bed."

"It's Mum."

"Has she got worse?"

"She passed away last night in her sleep."

There was a deafening silence as Lindiwe dragged herself out of bed, muffling her screams in her sleeve. She paced up and down as she tried to control herself.

"I thought you said she was going through some tests."

"Dad's a mess. Did I tell you? He's in hospital now. I think it's Covid. The doctors said Mum was positive in the end. Dad's blood pressure levels are off the charts! Lindiwe, I'm terrified."

"I feel so far away and helpless. What can I do?"

"I'm beginning to sound like an old record, but all you can do is send more money to help with funeral expenses. The funeral parlour takes care of everything since Dad's policy payments are up to date. But we still need to cater for our relatives and Mum's church people who will come home in droves to pay their condolences."

"Even when they know Mum died of Covid? I thought people were being discouraged from assembling. I know of three people who died recently after attending a funeral; the deceased, his son, and the priest who conducted the burial ceremony. It's awful. Have either of you been tested?"

"Dad has been tested now that he's in hospital. He was in complete denial and the number one conspiracy theorist, and unfortunately, he is not the only one. I admit I had been putting off testing for some time. Now, I'm waiting for the results. Covid is big business here — part of the money you sent I used for my test, and I couldn't afford the cost before my payday. It's US $60 a pop."

"That's crazy! We get tested regularly at work, and we are even at the front of the line for the new vaccine. I don't pay a cent, and it doesn't seem fair."

"We're a long way from getting free tests and vaccines. Even if they were available, someone would want to make people pay."

"Let's hope you're not positive," said Lindiwe. Are you experiencing any symptoms?"

"It's not winter, yet people have been suffering from flu-like symptoms. But I'm okay and just a little tired, with all the running around looking after Mum and Dad."

"Let me know when you get your results."

"Will you come home for Mum's funeral?"

"I can't, Maida, what with the quarantine restrictions and border closures. There's just no way. I'll send you money to set up a Zoom call. Our relatives and friends who can't travel would appreciate it. I'll keep phoning you for updates. Stay strong and please pass my love to Dad and tell him to get well soon."

The bitter winter days dragged on, and Lindiwe went back and forth to work like a robot. The passion was no longer in her. She thought she was suffering from seasonal affective disorder syndrome compounded by stress about the situation at home and feeling increasingly claustrophobic in her bedsit. Depressing text messages flowed in from various chat groups, and Maida even sent one or two. Lindiwe was being drawn further into a deep hole of depression, compounded by inadequate sleep.

One afternoon, she became too introspective and hoped a walk in the sunshine would lift her spirits. There was a common where she had seen dog walkers strolling with their charges scampering in wild circles of freedom in all-weather while mothers kept a watchful eye on their toddlers in the playground. The sub-zero temperatures hardened the ground leaving ice crystals on tree branches, while the snow continued falling in light white flakes. Patches of the lawns were covered in slush, especially where multiple feet had trodden along the grass. A frozen lake nearby was now devoid of birdlife that had migrated elsewhere. Lindiwe's cell phone began ringing as she walked. She paused to answer it. "Maida. I've just finished work and am taking a stroll. How are you, and is Dad out of the hospital?"

"Hallo Lindiwe, it's your cousin Ben."

"Long time and what a surprise! Why are you on Maida's phone?"

"I'm so sorry I don't know how to say this, but your father passed away last night. He never came off the ventilator. Maida had been staying at my mum's place since she'd been unwell lately. She received the news about your father, and the next thing we knew, she'd collapsed. It was all so sudden. My mum tried to revive her while I called an ambulance, but we were too late. I'm so sorry."

"This can't be! I talked to her only yesterday! How could she have deteriorated so quickly?"

"We honestly don't know. It must have been the shock, and I don't think Maida had fully recovered from the recent loss of your mum. When she phoned you, we were in the same room and overheard part of the conversation. Maida already had her positive test results by then. We kept nudging her to tell you that she was not well either. But she said you had enough to cope with, so we let her be."

"I need to get back to my flat. Thanks for calling Ben."

As she put her phone back in her coat pocket, Lindiwe wrapped her scarf more tightly around her neck and walked onto the lake's frozen surface. The thin ice cracked like shattered glass. She carried on wading, sinking, creating ripples under the ice until she disappeared without a trace.

Family Resolutions

"Aunty! Count down is still about eight hours to go."

"How lovely to hear your voice Chenai! I had planned to catch up with you after the festive season. How was your Christmas Day?"

"Same old, same old." I paused the TV remote. "We had a real spread at Mum's place with the usual crowd around the table, trying not to tread on each other's toes. There was enough food to feed an army. All is well at this end. Is everything okay with you? You sound strained."

"I didn't want to bother you, but I slipped on a bathroom mat yesterday."

"Oh, no! Are you in pain?"

"I'm in the hospital for observations till tomorrow. Covered in bruises, of course. My doctor said I should be out probably tomorrow to recuperate at home."

"It sounds serious, Aunt Herriot. At least there are no broken bones. You should have phoned me."

"And spoilt your Christmas?"

"Aunt Herriot, you know I would've come round to see you, even over Christmas. When is visiting time?"

"East End Hospital's visiting time is 4-6 pm and 10-11 am. I am feeling much better."

"I'm not sure I can make it this evening. Has David been to see you? He should have told me."

"No, he hasn't been to visit."

"Aunt Herriot, is there something you're not telling me? What would prevent him from checking up on you, his mother?"

"We had an almighty quarrel. I haven't seen my son since Christmas Eve."

"What was the disagreement about this time?"

"It's the same as always. David blew his allowance with friends. Now he says he's broke, and he's behind on his rent and wants a loan. Since his father passed away, my son has been nothing but trouble. When he is clean out of money, he remembers he has a mother. I told him I'd had enough. What was his response? After forcing me to endure a bout of his verbal diarrhoea, he slammed the door and left. Ungrateful child!"

"That's awful, Aunt Herriot. So, he doesn't know that you're in the hospital? Let me try and talk some sense into him. Surely, he'll at least come and see you?"

"Good luck with that approach. I know my son, and I've tried my best as a mother. He doesn't think of others, and it's always about him and his needs."

"I feel for you, Aunty. So, I suppose this is not the time to talk about your planned relocation? David should never have left you alone in such a great big house."

"He wanted his space and didn't want his mother breathing down his neck."

I replied, "He could have lived with you and slept in a different ensuite bedroom for a week and probably still not even bumped into you."

I am not judgemental, but I have lost count of times my mother lamented over how his parents had enabled David, the product of a child born in old age. I'm not saying I don't have my faults, but he has taken recklessness to new levels since his teenage years: wrecking his first car, flunking college exams, and generally behaving like a spoilt brat. So, it wasn't a surprise to hear that mother and son were no longer on speaking terms. David was unemployed, with no interest in the family car dealership except as a cash cow. Aunt Herriot constantly reminded David about all his father's hard work in amassing their wealth. After only a few years, her large house and David's flat were the only debt-free assets left in her name. My parents had given up talking sense into her about living within her means. They berated me for involving myself in Aunty's affairs when she had a son who should take up his responsibilities.

That evening before her hospital discharge, I relented and decided to see my aunt. I couldn't keep the house sale paperwork on hold much longer.

"Chenai! Are these flowers for me? Thank you for coming even though you've lots to do before you transfer. I am feeling much better and ready to go home. The doctor is doing the rounds later this evening, and I hope he will give me the all-clear. However, I have a small problem."

"Is it anything I can help with?"

"I'm not sure I can cope with selling the house and starting afresh somewhere else. I don't have the energy and have so many happy memories of family life in my home, including David playing in the garden with his friends when he was younger."

"Aunty, sorry to sound rather short, but we've talked about this before. I thought we had agreed that your family business is experiencing a downturn. So, you can't afford to maintain the house, especially since you have no other income source. I even suggested that you sell the flat that David is living in, and the proceeds could help finance the family home. David could move back and live with you. You can't cope on your own, Aunty, and this recent fall is an example."

"Stop right there, Chenai. I'm not having David under the same roof again! You want us to kill each other?"

"So, what's the solution, Aunty? I can't force you to decide, but we can't keep flipping back and forth. I have a deadline and need to get the paperwork in by New Year's Eve and before leaving town. It's not about my commission; the place at Zuva Aged Care – the one with the tennis court and the pool – they won't hold it for you. Have you forgotten how much you loved that unit and the facilities?"

"Enough of your sales talk. Selling houses is clearly in your blood! The aged care home has more amenities than I would ever need. But what if I don't make any friends? What will I do with the excess furniture and my other personal belongings when I must downsize?"

"Okay, we'll go through the options again, Aunty. Do you remember how long it took to call an ambulance when you had your previous fall? That should have been a wake-up call. In Zuva, you will have panic buttons and medical help nearby." Aunty remained silent as Chenai continued, "Wasn't it you that remarked that your house looks dilapidated? It needs renovating, and David is sure not going to do it."

Aunty appeared deep in thought. "But the business…"

"Aunty, even your late husband wouldn't have been able to manage the kind of miracle needed to resurrect it in the current climate."

As if she hadn't heard Chenai, she continued, "If only David could turn our business around."

"After the sale of your mansion, you could even visit your sister in South Africa or upgrade your car. As for worrying about not making friends, I can't imagine that happening, especially if you put your mind to it."

"You really want this sale, don't you?" she said with a facetious smirk. "You do realise that after a death in the family, moving house is one of the most stressful life events?"

"I do understand, and I'm not that mercenary. However, if I leave without sorting out your estate, the aged care unit deal will fall through."

"My dear niece, I appreciate that you didn't come here to raise my blood pressure. I'll contact you as soon as I'm home and finalise my plans. As for David, God knows he's my only child and much as he annoys me, somehow, we have to make the relationship work."

I passed by David's flat after the hospital visit. He greeted me with his usual affectionate bear hug and broad grin, while hastily shifting papers and cushions to make room for me.

"Yes, Chenai! Long time! How's life?"

"I keep forgetting what a lovely flat you have! If it were on the market, it would cost a fortune. I like the beard, and it suits you. Whenever I visit your mum, you are never home."

"Sounds ominous. Did Mum send you? Because if she did, I don't want to hear whatever the message is."

"You haven't given me time to breathe, and you're already chasing me out. Did you know your mum had a fall?"

"No! When did this happen? Is she okay?"

"Yes, she is in East End Hospital and hopefully will be out tomorrow. David, whatever has happened between the two of you, you must be the bigger person."

"Why am I always the one to give in? You don't even know what the quarrel was about. Already you are taking her side."

"It's not my place to take sides, David. You can tell me it's none of my business, but your mum is also my aunt. She filled me in on your disagreement. Someone must look out for her, so please give her a break. Underneath all that bravado, she has taken the loss of your dad very badly."

"And I haven't? Mum is stubborn and doesn't listen to reason."

"You are also not always the most empathetic person. When she's down, she says all you think of is inheriting her money and that you are deliberately driving her to an early grave with worry."

"Mum's such a drama queen. I don't have any sympathy for her sometimes. I'm in dire straits, yet she sits on a large empty property. Mum's not prepared to sell and share the proceeds. She can't even maintain the place, and I certainly don't want to live there."

"It also doesn't help when you both can't talk like sensible adults. Grow up, David, and stop acting like a spoilt child."

"I'm not to blame."

"Okay. So can I count on you to have a civilised conversation about new accommodation arrangements for her in the New Year?"

"What's the hurry?"

"There is a small two-bedroom unit in an aged care home in my portfolio, and the deal must be signed before midnight on New Year's Eve. Your mum had tentatively agreed to move, and I'll help sell her current house. You can then talk to her about helping you out financially, and that's the deal."

"She's broke?"

"You, of all people, should realise she's stressed about finances, which probably explains your bust-up. Living alone, especially after her fall, is also not viable."

"Sounds like you've done most of the hard work of persuading her, and all I have to do is help her sign on the dotted line."

"I'm not being mercenary, David, but your mum isn't getting any younger, nor are you. Yet you're still shirking your…"

"Who made you the prefect?" David teased. "Give me some credit, my dear cousin. I'm sorry she's in hospital. Although I haven't talked to Mum, I've been thinking of living in the guest cottage where we'll be out of each other's hair. Then she won't have to move."

"There you go! That wasn't painful, was it?" said Chenai smiling, "I'm losing out on my commission, but it sounds like this could be a win-win year for everyone!"

Best Friends Forever

"Jessie, if you're not going to tell me why you invited me here, I'm off."

"Hold on, Sandy, now Godfrey's gone out; we can talk."

"Whatever it is, just spit it out!"

Jessie sat opposite, uncharacteristically still in her dressing-gown, nursing a half-empty coffee cup. Sandy sensed a hidden strain as she glanced around the room with a visible layer of dust and crumbs ground into the carpet.

The tension between Jessie and Godfrey over breakfast had been palpable, and Sandy resolved to bite her tongue till Jessie told her the whole story.

"My sixth sense tells me I will not like what I am about to hear," said Sandy.

"It's partly your fault, you know. You are the one who encouraged me."

"What do you mean it's my fault?"

"Remember my moaning about my marital boredom and Godfrey coming and going as he pleases. You said I should find something to occupy myself and take up a hobby, and I did. I joined a book club!"

"Good for you. So, what's the problem? Where's this story going?" Sandy continued, "Let me guess, you joined my book club while I was away? The one run by your ex-Baily? This story isn't going to end well."

"I thought you'd be pleased."

"I can sense tension, and Godfrey's not his usual self. How did he take your new hobby?"

"I'm about to fill you in!"

"This is taking forever, Jessie. Just to let you know, Godfrey phoned me recently, being rather cryptic and asking about the book club. He couldn't understand your sudden literary enthusiasm. He says you're always on the phone texting your group, and he was fishing for information."

"I'll admit it's a lively crowd and entertaining."

"Is that all it is? Did you tell him that Bailey is the convener?" said Sandy, taking Jessie's empty cup to the sink. "We are talking about Godfrey, my cousin, who's known you since high school and knows all your ex-boyfriends."

"Sandy, it's all right for you. You have a social life."

"Spicing up your marriage by socialising with your ex-boyfriend on the sly is your solution?"

"It's not as if Godfrey has accused me of anything. It's just I've been rather careless and..."

"Don't tell me more, Jessie. I'd rather you didn't involve me in your secrets. I'm not the one who encouraged you to get married so young."

"Now, you are being both catty and unfair. My marriage was wonderful initially, and we used to have fun date nights. Your cousin only had eyes for me, but with this recent promotion, all he does is work."

"To provide for life, you're now accustomed to! It's not about blame. You want me to be one of your cheerleaders, but I don't want to be caught in the middle, Jessie. You know Bailey has never got over you."

"I know. You don't need to remind me. What's wrong with still having feelings for an old flame?"

"Knowing you, you've been encouraging him. Hang on! When you stood me up at last week's after-work drinks, were you with Bailey? OMG, I can't believe I'm so naive! How do you think my cousin will react if he ever finds out? He'll think I encouraged you. Who doesn't know your past with Bailey?"

"Don't be so melodramatic, Sandy. I know how protective you are of Godfrey, and yes, I was tempted for a short while."

"Jessie!"

"I love Godfrey, and he shouldn't feel threatened by some harmless flirting. It's only a bit of fun! God knows I could do with some!"

"A bit of fun? Don't tell me you don't see how Bailey looks at you whenever we are in his company."

"That's part of the fun and excitement!"

"You've forgotten Godfrey's parents are still in the middle of a messy divorce?"

"Okay. Okay. But I do have unfinished business with him. You remember how messed up I was when he dumped me, and I spent all my time moping around in your flat."

"You must let go, Jessie. You are married now! All I'm saying is that the days of acting like an impressionable schoolgirl are over. Godfrey loves you, and he shouldn't go through his current family traumas alone."

"Now that's unfair, Sandy. You make it sound as if I'm self-absorbed."

"Don't look for happiness in the wrong places and drop the book club! I'm in your corner Jessie."

"Okay! I've heard you, Sandy, but what's this rumour about you and some married sugar daddy politician who's set you up in the Avenues?"

"You asked me to come and discuss your issues, remember."

"Not so fast, my friend. Is it true that..."?

"Wow, Jessie, is that the time? I'm already late for my meet up. Say hi to Godfrey."

Sandy gave Jessie a quick hug, smiled while tapping her nose and left.

The Reunion

Life at Shamwari Old People's Home had its routines. Having completed the morning duty roster, the residents would sit in the shade for most of the day.

"Breakfast was late again today," said Botoro.

"You call that breakfast? The porridge had weevils. Black tea and stale bread!"

Wireless picked up his stool and walking stick, scowled and interrupted Sixpence's rant, "You're always complaining about something. Go and live elsewhere."

"You two," said Botoro, "I'm tired of being your referee. How do you share a room at night with this endless bickering? You both know we've nowhere else to go."

Despite the superintendent's persistent warnings about the health risks of smoking raw tobacco, the three carried on basking in the sun, puffing away on their homemade rolled cigarettes with guiltless self-indulgence.

Botoro changed the subject, "Wireless, my friend, have you heard from your daughter in Harare?"

"How many do you have?" said Sixpence.

"One that I know of," said Wireless, scratching the ground with a twig.

"You're lucky you even have one," said Botoro. "I lost touch with my family a long time ago, and I've no one to blame but myself after deserting them when I went looking for work."

Wireless sat up, "You never returned to your village in Malawi, Botoro?"

"Initially, I joined a group of gold panners in Zimbabwe as we swarmed like locusts invading an area covering fifty kilometres near the border. A wily old chief who was the landowner evicted us when he realised he was sitting on a lucrative venture. From then on, I spent years drifting from one job to another, enjoying single, unencumbered life."

Now 78 years old, Botoro had spent three years at Shamwari Old People's Home and become institutionalised. He had neither the energy nor wherewithal to care for himself. With no income to speak of, he relied on donations from well-wishers; a faded shirt here, a second-hand pair of trousers there. Together with Sixpence and Wireless, they had been brought to the home a few months apart after being picked up as vagrants by local police. Sixpence and Wireless had been lucky to be assigned one-room accommodation in the complex, whilst Botoro shared the men's dormitory with total strangers.

That Friday, the superintendent had finally succumbed to Botoro's persistent request to be escorted to follow up on his case at the government offices. Even his friends were tired of the endless stories of the planned reunion with Botoro's family.

"I don't want to spend my remaining days in unfamiliar surroundings. There may be no relatives left in my village, having moved on, but I don't want to die not knowing, like Samatia," said Botoro.

"Yes, that was tragic," said the superintendent. "We had to give him a pauper's burial."

"Don't get me wrong," said Botoro, "I'm grateful for a roof over my head, but we all can see that the home is underfunded and struggling to give us a decent quality of life."

The Department of Services Office was a distance from the home, and the trip took longer than expected because the home's truck decided to develop an oil leak that day. Using public transport to complete the journey, Botoro and the superintendent arrived at the government office, where a young officer greeted them with a nod. The officer looking wet behind the ears did not instil confidence. From experience, Botoro knew these low-level paper-pushers tended to demand rather than earn respect.

Botoro introduced himself while the officer, with the name tag 'Mr Nhamo,' fumbled through a heap of disorganised, dusty papers on his desk, looking for his case notes. He then started doodling on his desk pad, anticipating a long narrative. However, Botoro remained silent, unintimidated. Mr Nhamo eventually stopped fidgeting with his cell phone and looked at the older man dressed in an old-fashioned brown suit and tie, which had seen better days. Botoro finally piqued Mr Nhamo's interest, "Mr Botoro, speak slowly and clearly. You say you submitted appeals before, asking to find your family, yet there's nothing on file."

After searching through a filing cabinet jammed with yet more files and then phoning his superior to ask what to do about the missing documents, the officer turned to Botoro, "We can't find the letter you claim you sent to this department."

Bororo glanced at the superintendent, who was adamant, "The letter was hand-delivered, date stamped on receipt, and signed for only last week. Unfortunately, I didn't come with my file copy."

"That's unfortunate," said Mr Nhamo. "Our copy could have been misfiled. My supervisor says that we can initiate the process without the missing letter to make progress, so you don't have to wait until it shows up. You say you've lost touch. How does one lose a family, Mr Botoro? You are an African, and we have relatives everywhere, people of your totem or clan members."

Botoro began to feel dejected. This was not a good start. "My son, my name is Emmanuel Botoro, and I came to this country as a migrant. I was born near Blantyre in Malawi. My parents were poor peasant farmers, so I never attended school because they couldn't afford the fees and wanted me to work on our family plot. As the firstborn among three boys and one girl, we survived by selling seasonal produce at the local market."

The official glanced at his watch, saying, "Mr Botoro, I'm sure all you are saying is relevant but just give me the key facts."

The superintendent patted Botoro on the shoulder reassuringly as he continued, "I worked on various farms until I got married traditionally. Then, I lost my job after my wife had a son. With no steady income, we started experiencing marital problems. My wife then left abruptly for her rural home with my son."

The officer toyed with his pen before looking up, "So you know where she is?"

"No, that's my problem! I know where she was born, said Botoro, "but I haven't tried to find her since she left me—a question of pride. I was too ashamed to meet my in-laws after neglecting them. It was such a long time ago, and we migrants are transient people. My small savings soon ran out before I started sleeping rough. Eventually, the police picked me up and accused me of vagrancy. That's how I ended up in the old people's home."

"Any other relatives in Zimbabwe?"

"I lost contact with my uncle soon after I arrived. I wish to meet up with my family back home and not die in Zimbabwe but in Malawi. I was last there nearly 50 years ago, and I am sure my clan would still welcome me. That's my story."

Botoro, weary after his lengthy narrative, sat in the prevailing silence as the officer completed his notes in longhand. Mr Nhamo realised that this could be the story of his father or even a relative.

"I've written your story in full, Mr Botoro, and I can assure you that we will not lose your notes this time. Give us time to connect with our counterparts in the District Offices near the village where your wife's family comes from. If we can't find them, then we can talk about repatriation to your homeland, although I would be surprised if anyone you know is still alive. Leave the matter with me. Give me a week or two."

Botoro and the superintendent returned to the home, exhausted yet feeling a sense of accomplishment. Botoro relished the attention in the dormitory as everyone gathered around to hear the embellished report of his outing.

Sixpence said, "Was it just a chance to get out of this place?" The others laughed.

"Our truck broke down, and my documents have been mislaid," said Botoro.

"Tell us something new," said Wireless rolling his cigarette," the last time I was in that vehicle, it had a flat tyre on our way to the clinic. We had to wave a local farmer down to give us a lift."

"Wireless, you want to get us into trouble again over smoking in the dorms? You think I don't know you are the one chucking cigarette butts under my bed."

"Wireless, Sixpence, do you want to hear about my trip? If you don't, the others do," said Botoro.

"As long as it is not the long-winded version," said Sixpence, as the others chuckled.

After narrating his story, Botoro concluded, "I hope they find my family, especially my son." The supper gong could be heard in the distance as Boroto's audience drifted off, murmuring about raising false hopes. After all, Government offices were notorious for losing paperwork. If they have done it once before, why not again?

Botoro was the centre of attention for a week or two, but interest soon waned as new tales surfaced about Hilda, a new woman resident.

"You're now old news, Botoro," said Wireless in between puffs of tobacco.

"You have to keep up with the latest, my friend," said Sixpence. "Some say Hilda's story is even more pathetic than most if one believes the grapevine. She was dumped here by her daughter."

"That's unheard of. It'll bring that daughter bad luck, and it's against the cultural norms," said Wireless. "Children should look after their parents."

Botoro didn't join in the gloating about Hilda's misfortunes, saying somebody should help her resolve her family's quarrels. Despite ongoing niggling concerns, he continued with his daily routine. Occasionally, when Botoro enquired about progress in his case, the answer was always negative.

One morning Botoro paid yet another visit to the superintendent's office. He enquired with cap in hand while standing at the door, "Have you heard anything? The young officer at the Department of Services, do you think he's doing anything about my case?"

"Come in and take a seat," said the superintendent.

"Do you think my reports have been lost yet again?"

"Botoro, I don't know, but I can call the offices again."

"Mr Nhamo may have been transferred and replaced by someone with no sense of urgency in my case," said Botoro.

One morning after three weeks of waiting, the superintendent approached Botoro, weeding in the vegetable garden. The news was mixed.

"First, the bad news, I am sorry to tell you that your estranged wife passed away a few years ago. My sincere condolences." The superintendent stood awkwardly over Botoro, bent over his hoe.

The older man stared at the newly dug soil and asked, with watery eyes, "What about my son Givemore?"

"That's the good news, Botoro. Your son stayed with his grandparents, and they didn't know you were still alive. He wants to meet you." The superintendent quickly grabbed Botoro, who became weak at the knees and was about to collapse.

"Leave the weeding for now," urged the superintendent. "The news is a lot to absorb all at once. Go, rest and celebrate with your friends."

The night before Givemore's visit, Botoro was excited, chatting about the reunion among his friends Wireless and Sixpence while roasting maize and sweet potatoes around an open fire.

"You'll get a stomach-ache eating undercooked things, Sixpence. Then you'll blame it on the home's kitchen. Leave the maize in the cinders for a bit longer. You can't be that hungry. We've only just had supper," said Wireless.

"You're teaching me how to roast maize at my time of life? Don't you…"

Botoro said, "You two, why can't you have a decent conversation without quarrelling? Instead, you should be both advising me on my son's visit tomorrow."

"What's there to advise? You act naturally," said Sixpence.

"I wouldn't listen to him if I were you, Botoro. Remember, he's never raised children, and he's…"

"Here we go again! Can we stay focused on tomorrow? I am concerned about starting on the wrong foot, and I need your counsel. Would it be appropriate during the reunion to talk about forgiveness? Givemore now has his own family, and I want to be a grandfather to his children."

Wireless sounding solemn, said, "Aren't you jumping the gun? Have you thought about how your son feels about reuniting with a long-lost father?"

"I'm taking it for granted that he'll be just as happy as I am. I don't know. Have I left all this reconciliation too late? What if Givemore asks me why I never looked for him?"

"We can't answer for you, my friend," said Wireless.

The three talked late into the evening till the night watchman on his rounds advised them to extinguish the fire and go to sleep. Botoro lay awake in the dormitory with fears gnawing at him like undergrowth scorching in a bushfire. Why hadn't he searched for his wife and son earlier? Had he become so unconcerned about family during his philandering?

"Are you ready for your visitor? Today, your son is visiting, isn't it?" said the superintendent, who was intrigued by Botoro's case.

In the dormitory, a new arrival replied, "I didn't sleep a wink! Botoro was restless, talking in his sleep as he tossed and turned." They all laughed at Botoro's expense as he hid his embarrassment while searching for a decent shirt to wear.

"Today's the day," said Botoro. "Wouldn't you be anxious about meeting a son you haven't seen since he was a toddler?"

Wireless walked in and replied, "Botoro, you worry too much. It'll be all right. Remember the saying, 'blood is thicker than water.' You should be proud that Givemore is trying to get to know you. Some of us will never get the chance for such reunions, and I know I've burned my bridges with my daughter."

The rest of the morning was a haze as Botoro waited in anticipation, especially since no specific arrival time had been mentioned. The sun soared across the sky, blistering by mid-day, and then waning as the day ended. Dusk approached, and still, Botoro waited in the shade, stubbornly refusing food and drink. Weakened by hunger and thirst, he became surly. Wireless tried once or twice to get him to drink some water.

"Family is worth waiting for. Suppose my daughter was coming; I would hang in there, my friend."

Sixpence came and tried to crack a few jokes on the way from buying tobacco, but Botoro remained sullen. Even Wireless was now not holding out much hope. Sixpence returned and spoke briefly to Botoro, who complained about the insects and wondered whether this was some form of divine punishment for neglecting his family.

The evening floodlights in the complex came on one by one. The superintendent, on his rounds, approached the old man to end the vigil in the cold night temperature.

"Botoro, my friend," said the superintendent, "You'll catch a cold. Come inside where it's warm. We've already locked the main gate, and it's unlikely anyone will arrive this late in the day. Perhaps Givemore had to deal with an emergency. Come inside."

Botoro's stone-cold body remained slumped precariously under the msasa tree, waiting for a son who never came.

Change Of Direction

"What time are the guests coming this evening?" Mai asked, busy in the kitchen with her daughter Nyasha, putting the last-minute touches to the celebratory meal. Glued to the laptop screen, Baba was oblivious to the question.

"Is it 7 o'clock? Some people are bound to arrive early."

Realising she was speaking to herself, Mai raised her voice, "Aren't you supposed to be sorting the barbecue outside Baba? What are you still doing on your laptop? Close it, for goodness sake. You always leave everything to the last minute!"

"Don't fuss, woman! Nyasha, come and let's finalise this latest offer from one of our suppliers."

"Which one? I thought we responded yesterday," said Nyasha peering over her father's shoulder. "Didn't you get my email? Yesterday was the deadline."

"My inbox is full. Aah, here it is. I'm glad you are on top of this deal. We can't afford to lose the order. Once I've just finished responding to the rest of the work emails, you can help me with the barbecue. I've still one unopened from your brother

116

Itai who's landing in a few hours, so why write? What time are we supposed to pick him up from the airport, Mai?'

'Mid-afternoon. Itai sent you the flight itinerary way back, and did you even read it?" Mai patted Baba on the shoulder, "Are you listening to me? Baba?"

"I can't believe this is happening."

Wiping her hands on a dishtowel, Mai approached Baba's screen, "Why is Itai sending you such a long email anyway? Has flight arrival time changed? Where are my glasses?"

From: "itai mango" imango@gmail.com

To: "ben mango"<bmango@yahoo.com> Tue, 12 Apr at 10:18 am

Hi Mai and Baba

How's life? Have the rains come? I didn't mention one thing during our call last night since you both sounded so excited about my return. I've changed my mind and am not coming home right away, maybe later. I've also decided not to join the family business, even though Baba has plans for his imminent retirement.

"What is this son of yours talking about, Mai? Have I missed something since yesterday's phone call?"

"This son of *mine*? Baba, read the rest. Our son has more to say."

"Do I need to read any more? He isn't coming back. After all I've done for him. Is running one of the largest companies in the country not good enough for him? First, he doesn't want to get married, and now he wants to reject a well-paying job. Did you know anything about this? You are the one he talks to. I've always said you mollycoddle him. Now, if he had been…"

"Honestly, Baba! Read the rest of the email, and then you can comment. Let me sit so I can see properly."

I have secured a teaching post at my old university and will apply for tenure followed by dual citizenship. There is nothing back home for me. Sorry for the long email. I told Sis Nyasha my plans. She's enjoying working in the business. Your loving son

Itai

Mai started pacing behind her husband's chair, holding her head, "After all the preparations! What will I do with all this food?"

"Your food, Mai! There are more important things to worry about. What's got into Itai? How am I expected to retire? And why didn't he mention all this yesterday during his call?"

"You know full well that the call would not have ended well. Baba, you can be so pig-headed sometimes and melodramatic! A workaholic like you taking early retirement? That will be the day!"

As if he hadn't heard Mai, he turned to Nyasha, "My succession plan is up in smoke. Talk to your brother Itai. He must realise his priority should be his family."

"What's the point? He has made up his mind," said Nyasha. "Baba, you can't force him to take over a business he doesn't want."

Regaining his composure, Baba said, "That brother of yours could run it to the ground if he isn't interested, and it's probably my fault. I can't believe I didn't read the signs over the summer break. Itai was very attentive, but was he going through the motions to please me? I've put my heart and soul into the enterprise, no mean feat in this harsh economic climate. Tell me, who turns their back on such a profitable going concern and instead chooses to bury their head in books? I can never understand the youngsters of today."

Mai re-joined the conversation, "It's not as if you haven't a potential successor, and you don't have to sell the family business."

"You're way ahead of me. Whom can I groom at this late stage in my life?"

"Nyasha."

"Nyasha? Do you mean Nyasha, our daughter? You can't be serious. What happens when she gets married?"

"What would stop her even when she's married? Have you ever talked to her? I'm surprised you haven't considered her. Nyasha has been the backbone of your business since she started straight after completing her accountancy degree. I don't think you give her due credit, and she knows the operations like the back of her hand."

'It's one thing helping me out now and again. She's too quiet and not an extrovert like her brother Itai."

"Isn't she the one going head-to-head with our competitors? You already have a solid business plan, and she led the team which put it together. Nyasha is bright, already in situ and family. I'm surprised I even have to persuade you."

'As always, Mai, you've provided a solution I hadn't thought about. You women are...'

"Now, Baba, don't go and spoil it by making some sexist comment."

"I was going to say I'm around for a few more years, and I can start handing over the ropes to Nyasha. Slowly, slowly mind you! Who says a woman can't run a multi-country operation such as funeral parlours in this day and age?"

Lost Memories

As I tried to relax in Mai's lounge on the old black sofa with blue cushions sewn many years ago, my despondency weighed me down. My parents' black and white wedding photo hung on the wall in an old picture frame. Mai, my mother, was sitting beside me, no longer reflecting the youthful bloom of a blushing bride. Now a shell of her former self, she was silent while Tadiwa, her caregiver, fussed over her well-being and anticipated every need. Tadiwa had been filling a vacuum my sister Shylet and I had created by moving to the UK. We had never expected that Mai would ever need us as she did now.

After a long flight the day before, I arrived at Harare International Airport and approached the Immigration Desk with my completed entry forms. The Immigration Officer glanced at me and then over my documents.

"Chenai Katiyo?"

"Yes, that's me."

"Visitor or returning resident?"

"I'm visiting Mai Katiyo, my mother, just for a few weeks."

"Country of permanent residence?"

"Zimbabwe, although I'm currently living in London."

She gave a perfunctory smile and a parting comment before handing back my stamped passport. As I approached the baggage carousel to collect my suitcases, I felt a sense of relief, now on home soil. Coming to see Mai made me realise how homesick I had been.

No one was waiting to welcome me at the airport. That is the way I wanted it. Instead, I hailed an airport taxi which charged me $ US40, a rip-off for the short distance to Msasa Park. When I first entered the lounge, Tadiwa greeted me like a long lost relative, her conversation punctuated by numerous questions while Mai tried to understand what all the fuss was about. It eventually dawned on her as she stared at me. She was overcome with joy and tears as she embraced me while seated. I could sense that it was taking Mai some time to absorb the situation while Tadiwa, in her excitement, said, "Mai, don't you remember her? It's your daughter Chenai. She is here now. Say something!"

Mai stared at me, saying my name repeatedly in a whisper as she clutched my hand, stroking it incessantly.

After making Mai comfortable, Tadiwa joined me in the spare bedroom as I was unpacking my suitcase. In a low voice, she filled me in.

"I am so glad that you came. You can see Mai for yourself. I couldn't explain everything on the calls because she's not lost her hearing. The doctor you asked to do home visits explained her illness to me, an advanced form of dementia. All we can do is make her comfortable. That's all I am doing, really, and talking to her as we used to, even though she rarely responds. I am so relieved you are back!"

I unpacked a small parcel and handed it to Tadiwa. Overcome with emotion, I embraced her briefly and said in a faltering voice, "Tadiwa, if only you knew how inadequate I feel, giving you such a small token of our appreciation. If it were not for you, we would not be where we are. We have left you with Mai, and its no easy task looking after someone who can no longer communicate effectively what she wants or how she feels. My sister Shylet and I can never repay you."

Tadiwa opened the parcel of a yellow flowery summer dress and an envelope containing dollar bills, and she responded, "Chenai, I know how hard it is to find work in this country of ours. I'm so grateful that you employed me, and you trust me with your mother's life. When I have time off and the agency caregiver you arranged comes to relieve me, I feel disorientated because I have become so close to Mai. Thank you for paying me on time. Thank you for these gifts."

Tadiwa later joined us in the lounge for the rest of the evening as we feasted on traditional food interspersed with conversations about old and new stories. There was a constant stream of neighbours and family curious to meet Mai's prodigal daughter. Soon the buzz and conversations dried up together with the perfunctory cups of tea and refreshments. After excuses about unattended homes, homework supervision, and cooking meals, the visitors left. This deluge, I could sense, had been an ordeal for Mai, who hadn't said much the whole evening. Tadiwa ushered me to bed, saying I needed rest from my jet lag.

Before Mai's illness, she moved with Tadiwa into her compact two-bedroom house in Msasa Park. She was now one of the few remaining first buyers of the housing scheme built after Independence. You could always tell the difference between the homeowners with their smart well-kept houses and immaculate gardens, in contrast to those occupied by transient lodgers with skewed curtains, junk-filled yards and no lawns to speak of.

When Mai first moved in, she was so proud that she had a housewarming party in the backyard. My sister Shylet and I couldn't attend. However, pictures of the celebration were plastered on Facebook by one of Mai's nieces. After consuming copious quantities of alcohol and the proverbial celebratory meal of sadza, rice, chicken and coleslaw, everyone looked the worse for wear.

When Mai felt lonely, although she was not alone, we heard that she envied relatives and friends with children living in the country. They at least saw each other at weekends and during the holidays. Like her peers at family gatherings, she missed living with my sister and me and boasting about our accomplishments. After retirement from teaching, Baba, my father, had disappeared some years back, swept away by the euphoria of Independence. The last we heard of him were rumours that he had 'traded' in our mother and found a new model like others at that time—a new wife half his age. My mother never got over the affair.

Some years after Independence, I had left for the UK, followed by Shylet, who joined the exodus of yet more economic migrants looking for a better life. She worked as a caregiver for an old English spinster on a remote farm in rural Hampshire. Shylet never remarried after a disastrous union with her childhood sweetheart Jim who had emigrated with her. A typical Shona man with an ingrained strong rural background, he could not adjust to the UK's 'liberal' ways of life, where Shylet was treated as an equal under the law. Both worked full time with no maid, a luxury they had left back home. The marriage was doomed soon after Jim lost his job, which was way below his qualifications, and succumbed to drink and despair, leaving Shylet to fend for the family.

Shylet's UK immigration papers had not been valid for a while, so there was no way she would visit Mai anytime soon. She was initially an accounts student at a polytechnic with an obscure name and then ran out of money to pay for her course before overstaying her welcome. Now living under the radar, she was employed by whoever was willing to pay her below the tax barrier, helping perpetuate her illegal immigrant status. But Shylet never defaulted from sending money for Mai via Western Union. It was her way of coping with a nagging conscience over both of us being away from home and leaving Mai childless.

When my sibling and I came together at Mai's new house, the occasions had been few and far between. The last time was Easter, three years ago. That had been a mission, what with the exorbitant holiday airfares to Harare. We habitually spent lots of money on phone calls to Mai and eventually sent her a cell phone and communicated via WhatsApp. At 78 years, however, no matter how many times we told her how to retrieve the messages, the instructions went through one ear and out the other. She never learned to text back in response, saying it was too complicated and someone was bound to offer to read her messages. There were no secrets.

Despite my financial hardships, my conscience told me that I should go home and assess Mai's situation for myself. I always had a special bond with her, although we never talked of Mai having a favourite with my sister. Of late, my telephone calls to her had been leaving me unsettled. Sometimes I could hear in the background, Tadiwa prompting Mai and reminding her who I was before Mai gave up trying to understand. Instead, she would echo the standard answer to me, 'I am fine.' After the initial greetings, there was no meaningful conversation before she passed the phone on to Tadiwa. The irony was never lost on me that we cared for others in the diaspora while raising money to pay strangers who cared for our mother back home. I would occasionally end the conversation rather abruptly before dissolving into tears at the futility of the calls. Concern for my mother from such a distance seemed self-indulging. My two consolations were that at least I could send remittance back home, and Tadiwa was doing her best. Even then, a niggling feeling would occasionally envelop me, and I would sink into a low level of depression. Money and material things were no substitute for my being at home with Mai.

So, during this visit, I had extended my holiday, having applied for unpaid leave, which I could ill afford. One could also not arrive empty-handed, with all the relatives to see, including those in the rural areas. Mai always had a long list of all the people we were obliged to visit—passing condolences for all the missed funerals, congratulating those with new additions to the extended family, leaving a parcel or cash with expectant relatives. Little did they know that both Shylet and I were working more than one job and sometimes survived on one meal a day to raise the cash so we could arrive back home, the 'successful ones' from the diaspora. Well-meaning friends would advise, why not just send your mother the money for her needs and those of the hangers-on? The sum would undoubtedly be far less than the airfares. People want money for school fees, medical bills, groceries, and the like, not parcels of discount clothes that they could easily buy from the local flea markets.

As the days passed, I soon caught up on Mai's welfare as Tadiwa opened up, mentioning that visitors and relatives who used to go in and out of Mai's house like a railway station no longer came. The caregiver reported that no one ever revealed they felt uncomfortable seeing Mai in an increasingly lethargic state, unable to recall the time or day of the week. Instead, they behaved as if they thought her dementia was infectious and it was better to stay away. Her hearing was still acute, and there were fleeting moments when one could sense some recognition and presence of her former self from her eyes.

My euphoria at being back home soon began to wear thin. There was no doubt that Mai was being looked after very well. She was clean, well-fed, albeit slightly overweight because she was no longer walking or keeping fit doing housework. She appeared comfortable, and the pantry was full. However, I could sense Mai's health was deteriorating. She was no longer able to dress or bathe herself. The disorders affecting her brain were taking their toll. Even Tadiwa, the eternal optimist, said that Mai was not herself anymore. Her monotonous pastimes were now sitting in her wheelchair, gazing in the distance, head in a lopsided manner. All day in the verandah, she chased the sun, day in and day out. If no one moved her chair into the shade, she would suffer from sunburn. When she was not dozing, I would sometimes join her and try and start a conversation.

"Mai, Mai. Can you hear me? I didn't want to wake you earlier. You had some visitors from the Mothers Union. You remember your friends whom you used to meet at church. The ones in the choir?" I paused, looking for signs that she was following what I was saying. She looked at me blankly.

I continued, "They came in smart uniforms like yours and brought groceries. On Sunday, when I went to the morning service, they mentioned visiting and saying a few prayers. They didn't sing your favourite hymns this time, we were afraid to wake you since Tadiwa says you didn't sleep well last night."

I sensed she had heard me as Mai turned her head and stared through me into the distance.

Gone were her flashbacks on the poor state of rural hospitals, reminiscing about when she was Sister in Charge at Nhowe Mission or my father's days as a promising head-teacher before Independence. In a slurred voice, she could still respond

132

sporadically to greetings after being prompted, limiting her conversations. Before leaving her for the UK, I wanted to share so many memories about life. I remembered the time we stayed with her mother in the rural areas. As children, we slept with my cousins, all squashed in one bed, talking in whispers through the night. I also recalled when Mai used to keep chickens and sell eggs to make ends meet. She had always been industrious. Even with a regular salary before retirement, she would sew maids and children's uniforms for sale at the Mission.

The mother in front of me was not the mother I knew. Alzheimer's held her hostage as she dozed in and out of her world. Even the energy to lift her arms and greet people with a handshake had now faded away. She reminded me of a new-born baby who ate and slept, ate, and slept. The only difference was that Mai was not growing up; she was not crying for attention. She was just there, with her closeted memories on a journey where none of us could accompany her. I had come too late. She was now lost to us all, forever.

When Rachel met Lucy

Sam stormed in and threw his coat on the sofa, slamming the door behind him. Rachel looked up from her novel as Sam flopped down on his discarded coat.

"You keep saying you want to meet my family."

"Hello Sam, I guess you've had an exhausting day," said Rachel trying to prompt some civility.

"I bought airline tickets online at work," Sam said, "we're leaving in three weeks."

After recovering from her initial surprise, Rachel said, "Three weeks? That doesn't give us much time. Why the rush?"

Sam let out a frustrated growl, "You keep saying I'm putting off this visit. Now you say the timing is inconvenient? Fine! I'll postpone it. I'll call my parents back and tell them that Rachel doesn't want to go right now." He got his phone from his pocket, muttering, "Can't afford to be going away now anyhow. It's not as if I was in a hurry to see them. I went last year."

"It's not about the money," Rachel began and immediately regretted it.

"Yes, because we're just made of money, aren't we? That's why you cancelled that joint trip to France with your folks. It wasn't because we can't afford it, but you'd rather not spend time with your parents."

"Don't be silly, Sam." She got up and headed across to the sofa to sit closer to him. "You know I enjoy spending time with my family, so I'm confused about why we don't get to spend any time with yours. Your reluctance is baffling. Have you told them about me?"

Sam and Rachel had studied at the same local community college for three years. He initially thought Rachel wasn't interested in him when they first met in a local student bar where a multiracial crowd congregated after lectures every Friday night. Sam had gone reluctantly one evening, sensing his friends were beginning to tire of him continuously declining to join them for even one drink. Soon after a short courtship, Sam and Rachel got married in a low-key registry wedding. None of his family attended, and he made excuses about the expense of flying from Zimbabwe to London.

When communicating with people back home, Sam painted a positive picture of someone who had settled well into his new life in London. About his homesickness and Rachel, he was more reticent. It was difficult to explain his experiences and sense of alienation and loneliness in a foreign land because none of his immediate family had ever lived through it.

There were occasional visits to Rachel's parents where Sam deliberately steered clear of any potentially controversial topics. He deflected prolonged conversations about his country of origin, saying little about his family.

Three weeks later, Sam arrived with Rachel at Harare International Airport. Sam emerged filled with emotion as he walked out of the arrivals lounge into the glorious midday sun. He was immediately recognised and surrounded by waiting relatives. Rachel, although excited, began feeling overwhelmed by the new experiences and stood at a distance observing the mayhem. Sam was relishing the attention from family members before he realised, she was standing apart. He entreated her to join him, witness and appreciate the songs and dances of welcome, interspersed with laughter and embraces. The celebration tempered as Sam introduced Rachel to Isaac, his brother, and the extended family. A young dreadlocked nephew, in his exuberance, asked with a fake American English accent, "Sorry, I missed the introductions in all the commotion. Did you say this is your wife?"

Sam responded briefly and deflected any further questions by rallying everyone saying, "We are exhausted, and I want to see my parents. Where's the transport? Let's go. Let's go!"

The group piled into a minivan which was soon jam-packed. It began heading down the highway to Greendale, one of the leafy suburbs of Harare. The noise levels were starting to overawe Rachel as everyone interrupted each other without pausing. Sam joined in, conducting a high-pitched conversation in his mother tongue, while others took furtive glances at Rachel in the front seat. She was squashed between Sam and the minivan's driver, bobbing his head to the beat of loud throbbing music from the car radio. Oblivious to her fellow passengers' lively conversations, she looked out at the bustling life along the route as the driver weaved through the traffic at breakneck speed. The afternoon's dry heat and feelings of nausea compounded by jet lag had now resulted in a tense, nervous headache.

On arrival at the parents' house, the minivan parked near the front door and the occupants poured out. Sam saw his parents, Baba, and Mai, rising from their garden chairs on the verandah. They slowly approached him in welcome. With pure white hair peeking from under a checked brown cap, his father wore his grey safari suit for special occasions. It was now shiny with age. Baba could, however, still walk confidently with an air of pride. Behind him came Sam's mother stooping over a wooden walking stick, dressed in a multicoloured African print, her smile beaming. Sam embraced them in turn as if they were fragile dolls.

On realising there was one face he didn't recognise among the throng, his father turned in expectation to Sam, trying to catch his eye. Sam reverted to his mother tongue as he drew Rachel close.

"Mai and Baba, this is Rachel, my wife." There was an awkward pause. Sam continued, "Let's go inside and go through the formalities. We are exhausted! I hope Mai has cooked my favourite meal, *sadza, tsunga rine dovi ne kanyama.*" Turning to Rachel, he said, "It's our staple food of stiff porridge, green vegetable leaves with peanut butter and meat. You will enjoy it, Rachel!"

Sam guided his parents into their lounge and sat down as they continued staring at him in puzzlement and awe. After getting their breath back and completing the welcome formalities, the family served Sam's favourite meal. The small talk was a mixture of English and Shona, so Rachel would not feel excluded. After exhausting topics about the ongoing heatwave and impending drought, the neighbours and the journey, Sam's father, with watery deep-set eyes, finally turned to his son and in Shona said, "Sam, it's wonderful to see you. You're coming home has made us very happy. We've been praying for your safe return since you left. Introduce us properly. Who is the person seated next to you? We were not expecting anyone to come with you. Is it a friend or what? Of course, she is welcome."

His father and mother looking perplexed, waited for an answer. Rachel sitting next to Sam, could feel their intense gaze. She sensed they were talking about her and recognised that the mood was now more sombre. Sam's mother had not uttered a word after the initial greetings, as if she was not part of the conversation. Rachel nevertheless could feel her piercing brown eyes.

Initially, Sam, lost for words, though he had envisaged this tension would exist, tried to imagine what was going through his parents' minds. He was their firstborn, whom they had sponsored to study locally in multiracial private schools and then supported his move to the UK. Had there not always been a possibility that Sam might make friends or even marry across the colour lines? The tension in the room was palpable as Sam started haltingly to narrate his story about Rachel and how she had become his wife.

In barely a whisper, Sam said, "I can tell you're shocked and disappointed that I didn't inform you before marrying Rachel."

"Marriage is about bringing families together, my son," said his father. "You've deprived the immediate and extended family of their traditional role in the process."

"Rachel wouldn't have appreciated the significance of half our traditions anyway," said Sam belligerently.

"But my son, you've chosen what you want from Rachel's culture, was she given the same opportunity to embrace ours?"

His mother added, "I hope you married her for the right reasons."

"What does that even mean, Mai?"

"We've heard stories of marriage as a means to a better life abroad or for immigration papers. Those are just a few of the perceptions people in our community have around interracial relationships," said Mai.

Sam interrupted, "I can't believe I'm hearing this from my own parents! What do you take me for?"

"We love you, Sam," said his father, "but don't forget that your mother and I still have memories of apartheid when intermarriage was taboo and those who persisted split families.

At one stage, such unions were even against the law. If we don't voice these worries with you, my son, who will?"

Sam calmed down, realising that the comments were out of anxiety and concern for him.

"I hear you, Mai, and Baba. My immigration papers are in order, and I didn't have to marry for citizenship. I'm also confident in myself and proud of who I am. Rachel and I married for love."

In the heat of the discussion, no one remembered to translate. Sam's father glanced at his wife, his thin lips quivering with emotion. She continued staring at her feet, her wrinkled hands clasping and unclasping. During the short lull, Sam's brother Isaac walked into the room and respectfully sat down near Sam, trying to gauge the mood of his parents and older brother. The father reverted to addressing Sam, "Today should be a day of celebration, and I stress we have no quarrel with Rachel. She probably comes from a respectable family. Did you pay a dowry for her, and who was your go-between, your *munyai?*"

"We didn't need to do all that, Baba. Once Rachel's parents accepted me, we had a small registry wedding. I can show you the pictures, and they are here somewhere…"

"We'll make time for all of that later. Are you planning to make your home here?"

"It's unlikely, Baba since we both have well-paying jobs back in London. We're only here for a short time, for you to meet Rachel and do a bit of sightseeing."

"It sounds like you've thought of everything," said Baba pensively. "However, have you forgotten about Lucy, the woman you left behind with marriage promises? The one we thought you'd pay *lobola*, her dowry? If you had married Lucy, my best friend's daughter, back in the village, your customary marriage would have further cemented our relationship."

"I'm confused. One minute you're saying you accept Rachel, yet you're still harping on about a childhood relationship that had run its course."

"You've moved on, Sam, but you left us behind," said Baba.

The mood of the homecoming celebration had changed irrevocably, and the strained conversation carried on through supper. As other senior family members arrived from the village to welcome Sam, his father explained the family's new situation. Their opinions mattered since marriage was not just about two individuals. Rachel, feeling somewhat neglected, quietly left the room and was now being entertained outside by the younger relatives who seized the opportunity to practise their English and ask about 'overseas'.

Back in the lounge where the elders had congregated, Mai raised her voice above the animated discussion for the first time that evening, "Baba, we've forgotten about our visitors arriving tomorrow in all the excitement."

"What visitors?" Sam looked from one parent to another.

"You're right, Mai. I'd completely forgotten!" His father continued, "Sam, when we heard you were coming, I told Lucy's father, my old friend, to come and join us in celebrating your safe return. He's arriving tomorrow together with Lucy, her mother and aunt."

"Are you telling me," said Sam, looking bewildered, "that Lucy and her family still have expectations?"

"Sam," said his mother. "How were we supposed to know that you had already taken another wife? All these secrets!"

"Mai, I thought we'd gone over this. I have a right to choose a wife."

"Rights! That's all we hear from you, youngsters. What's wrong with our traditions where everyone knows their place? Even Rachel…"

"Mum! Don't even go there. You're not giving Rachel a chance."

Baba sensed that the earlier friction was resurfacing, "My son, your mum, and I have accepted your decision. Mai, let's move on and discuss how to deal with Lucy's family."

The clan's meandering discussion finally concluded that Sam's father had some damage control to do. There was no going back once everyone understood that Rachel was Sam's legal wife under English law. Before resuming their celebration, the family agreed on a strategy to handle questions and awkwardness from any fallout. If Rachel and Sam stayed in Harare, no one back in the village would be the wiser. Rachel and Sam could spend the rest of their visit in far-flung tourist sites, Zimbabwe Ruins, Lake Kariba, and Victoria Falls. Sam could even take Rachel to Hwange Game Park since European tourists liked that sort of thing, wild animals in their natural habitat. A four-week holiday could fly past without any problems.

Rachel never visited Sam's rural home and the graves of his ancestors in the Eastern Highlands. After a thoroughly eventful holiday, the couple was ready to take their return flights to London, leaving any appeasements and intricacies of traditional customs for his parents and the clan to navigate.

A month later, the couple were in the departure lounge laden with curios from their trip when Rachel decided to visit a bookshop to pick up a local novel before boarding. Sam felt a tap on his shoulder.

"Sam, it is you. I didn't recognise you at first, with the beard."

"Lucy? Oh Lucy, how are you?" Sam drew Lucy away into a corner, a distance from where he'd been sitting. Furtively glancing around, he said, "What a surprise!"

"Long time! said Lucy smiling, "Did I startle you?"

"I'm sorry. I wasn't expecting to bump into you."

"I heard you were around."

"I got married, and Lucy, I'm sorry I never told you," Sam blurted out. "I know our parents had expectations about…"

"Those were their dreams, Sam. Is that why you seem on edge? I've known for a while about your new wife. A friend came across your wedding pictures on social media. Belated congratulations! Where is the lucky lady?"

Sam retrieved their luggage as Rachel approached, saying, "Sam, that's our flight. Are you ready?"

Lucy stepped back, saying in a low voice, "No hard feelings. Good luck!" She smiled, gave a little wave, and headed for her boarding gate.

"Who was that?" said Rachel as they boarded the plane.

"No one in particular. Just an old friend."

Chipo's baby

Natsai would never have admitted she was a hoarder. But since recently downsizing to a smaller flat, she realised she had accumulated a lot of excess personal effects. Brand new kitchen utensils and clothes were still in their original packs, unused. Books were her greatest weakness, and she had not read several of them and couldn't remember what had driven her to purchase or collect specific genres. Some, Natsai recalled, had been passed down by her much older sister Chipo who, in her restlessness and constantly being on the move, discarded possessions in her wake.

With limited space in her new flat, Natsai had cast sentimentality aside and decided to donate Chipo's old castoffs to a children's home, which had recently appealed for second-hand books for an upcoming fundraising jumble sale. As she sifted through a pile, a small, coloured photograph flew out of the back flap of one of the hard copies. Natsai turned it over, trying to make sense of the connection between the faces and the writing on the back in black ink. Cross-legged on the floor, she examined the photograph more intently. Although yellowing, the words

'The love of my life xxx' appeared to relate to a young woman holding a sleeping baby wrapped in a fluffy white blanket. The woman had a corkscrew coil hairstyle like Bob Marley in his younger days. She smiled with her head tilted while proudly holding up the baby slightly to the camera. Compared to the baby, the woman had a broad, attractive nose complimenting a rich brown skin tone, unlike her baby's paler complexion. Natsai concluded that it was a mother and child, and her fleeting yet strong resemblance suggested someone Natsai thought she knew.

Turning the photograph over again, Natsai thought there was a resemblance with her mother in her youth. But the baby was too young to identify, and if it was Chipo, her older sister, Natsai had never seen the photograph before.

As she took a break from unpacking, she rang Chipo.

"Hi Chipo, were you expecting another call? The speed you answered…."

"Oh, hello, little sister. Yes, I was expecting someone else. Is everything okay? How are you settling into your new apartment? How's the unpacking going?"

"Okay, so far. It looked bigger when it was empty! Not sure I will fit everything into this matchbox, and that's exactly why I'm calling you. Since I no longer have space, I'm getting rid of the old books you gave me. A small photograph fell out of one of them, and I'm assuming it must be yours. It's of a baby in the arms of someone who looks like Mum. Perhaps even..."

"I'm not sure which photograph you are talking about," said Chipo sounding wary, "so come over, and we can catch up and bring the picture."

When Natsai arrived, Chipo was sitting in her sun lounge with a small gin and tonic. After pecking Chipo on the cheek, Natsai sat down, looking concerned, "I thought you 've given up alcohol! Have you relapsed already? It can't have been more than one month of abstinence?"

Chipo brushed the comments aside, looking pensive with wrinkles furrowing her brow as her bloodshot eyes flitted across Natsai's face. There was also a lingering smell of cigarette smoke but no ashtray.

"Is this the photograph? Yes, I remember it now. That's me when I had just started working."

"Who is the baby?"

"It's a long story," said Chipo.

"That's what you usually say when you don't want to explain, Sis! If you don't feel comfortable talking about whatever it is, you don't have to. I was just surprised to find it among your books."

"As I said, it's a long story. Natsai, I'm not in a good place right now and would rather not open up old wounds. Let's talk about you. How's your new job? Mum says you've hit the ground running. Good for you!"

Natsai took the cue and shared her first week's experiences as a junior editor at a local newspaper. She had been thrown into the deep end with her first assignment on newly arrived refugees in her community. The photograph was not mentioned again.

A few weeks later, Natsai called in at her parents' place after her first paycheque, which she celebrated by buying lilies for her mother. Natsai decided against purchasing anything for her father, who was usually hard to please. Over a cup of tea accompanied by her mother's victoria sandwich cake, she said, "Mum, I had a strange conversation with Chipo recently. You know how she loves to talk. Anyway, she was rather cagey during my whole visit and fobbed me off with all sorts of topics, but not the one I wanted to hear about, this photograph I found among her old books. She says it's of her, but who is the baby?"

"Let me put my glasses on."

"Chipo gave me her old novels some time ago," Natsai said, "and this fell out. She didn't want to explain."

The parents passed the picture between them, looking at each other in silence. Natsai felt uncertain of what was coming next as her father put his newspaper aside.

She continued regardless, "Chipo looks much younger and happier than of late. But the baby, I have no idea, and babies at that age all look the same to me."

Father glanced at his wife and said gravely, "We've been putting off telling you for long enough."

"Darling," said Natsai's mother, "You need to sit down, and whatever we are going to tell you, please remember we kept it from you because we love you and thought it was for the best. We missed opportunities to discuss this as you grew up, and in the end, we were just too terrified that things would fall apart."

"Mum, Dad, you're making me scared. Just say it out! I am surely mature enough to handle whatever it is."

"The baby is you. You were a few months old."

"And it's Chipo holding me in her arms?"

"My love, yes, it is Chipo. She's…."

"The resemblance is there. But why do I feel you haven't told me everything?"

"It is a long story."

"If I hear that phrase one more time, I will scream! Someone tell me, is there some secret, and I'm the only one who doesn't know?"

"Natsai, Chipo is cradling you, as I mentioned before."

"And…?"

"Chipo is not your sister. She's your mother, and dad and I are your grandparents."

154

"Chipo is my mother?"

"Yes, darling. We've already told you too much, and Chipo should tell you her story," said the grandmother.

"You mean there's more? Why all these secrets from me?"

Her grandparents remained silent. Natsai retrieved the picture and left without saying another word.

The excitement of moving into the new flat quickly faded. Natsai kept herself busy after the bombshell, realising she didn't know her family. Chipo and her grandparents' phone calls went unanswered. Natsai, lounging in her pyjamas, unpacked her belongings while playing melancholy music. She opted to work from home and ordered her groceries online. Chipo resorted to leaving food parcels on Natsai's doorstep when her knocking was ignored.

"Chipo or I suppose I should call you Mum? I'm coming over, and your story had better be good, or I'll…"

"Oh, Natsai! I'm so pleased you phoned," said Chipo, "I've been so worried about you. When do you want to come? I am home all day, and we can eat out for lunch if you want."

"I hardly think there's anything to celebrate. I'm coming over in an hour."

Natsai arrived at Chipo's place, sidestepped the welcome hug, and went through to the verandah where a tray of iced mint and lemon drinks was on the table. She sat down and blurted out, "So when were you going to tell me?"

"Natsai, my darling, it's complicated."

"Today, I have all day for this 'complicated' story. I can't believe you and my grandparents kept me in the dark. Why?"

"Let me pour you a drink."

"There you go again, trying to postpone the inevitable. Chipo, I'm not a child, and I have a right to know. You told me you moved away from my grandparents when you were young, and then? I want to know about the picture and who my father is. No more secrets."

"We did it to protect you, Natsai," said Chipo, nervously fumbling in her pocket and then realising she had quit smoking.

"Protect me from what? How do you think I feel after discovering your 'secret'? If the photo had not fallen out, how long would you've have kept the pretence going, Mother?"

"You have a right to be angry with me, with all of us. I'm sorry. We honestly didn't think this through well enough; how we would tell you, when and life after the revelation."

"Well, now's the time to find out," said Natsai in a shaky voice.

"I was sent away to boarding school at 13, and it was the first time to stay so long away from my parents, especially as an only child. During the first few years, I enjoyed the experience and made friends, partly because my parents regularly came to visit, and I had plenty of pocket money. I don't know how I got mixed up with the wrong crowd during one holiday after a camping trip. One thing led to another, and the next thing I knew, I was pregnant with you at 15 years."

"You got raped?"

"No! No. Let's say I reaped the consequences of my choices. My parents and I agreed on home-schooling till I gave birth, and there was no question of adoption. Then I went to college to finish my studies."

"So why did you have to pass me off as your sister?"

"Times have changed, Natsai. Back then, having a child out of wedlock was a big deal, and we thought it best to hide my pregnancy from society. You forget your grandparents are prominent people in the community."

"You're saying it was better to lie to everyone, including me, than tell the truth?" Natsai disappeared into the house, leaving Chipo unsure whether she had said the right thing or made things worse.

Chipo heard running water in the bathroom and knocked, "Natsai, are you OK?"

"I'm coming."

"I'm so sorry, Natsai. Now that I've shared the story, I can see what you and others would think, that we were more concerned about appearances than your wellbeing."

As Natsai came out red-eyed, she blurted out, "You never wanted me. That is why you were hiding me from the world."

Chipo, embracing Natsai tightly, said, "You are wrong. I'm so proud of you. Every day I wanted to come out and explain but couldn't face the possible consequences. I'm glad the picture has forced us to tell the truth. I hope we can make up for lost time as mother and daughter."

As Chipo and Natsai took time to reconcile, Natsai looked at her mother one day and said, "It's funny calling you Mum. I suppose I'll eventually get used to it. There is still something you've not told me. Who is my father?"

"A parent's name is not added to a birth certificate unless they agree, and your father never knew I was pregnant because we would have been forced to marry, knowing his parents. Sadly, he died in a car accident a few years after you were born, and by then, the secret had taken a life of its own. But I know he would have loved you as much as he loved me. His name, however, I will take to my grave."

www.ingramcontent.com/pod-product-compliance
Lightning Source LLC
Chambersburg PA
CBHW071923130726
47909CB00014B/2564